D1366751

Pine and Punishment

Johnnie Alexander

AnniesFiction.com

Books in the Victorian Mansion Flower Shop Mysteries series

A Fatal Arrangement
Bloomed to Die
The Mistletoe Murder
My Dearly Depotted
Digging Up Secrets
Planted Evidence
Loot of All Evil
Pine and Punishment
Herbal Malady
Deadhead and Buried

. . . and more to come!

Pine and Punishment

Library of Congress-in-Publication Data
Pine and Punishment / by Johnnie Alexander
p. cm.
I. Title
2018935312

AnniesFiction.com
(800) 282-6643
Victorian Mansion Flower Shop Mysteries™
Series Creators: Shari Lohner, Janice Tate
Editor: Jane Haertel
Cover Illustrator: Bob Kayganich

10 11 12 13 14 | Printed in China | 9 8 7 6 5 4 3 2 1

1

Kaylee Bleu stepped back from the display window and appraised her work with a critical eye. A squat pine tree, cut from the woods behind Mary Bishop's home, occupied one side of the space. Gold lights twinkled amidst the branches, which were decorated with an assortment of miniature ornaments. Gaily wrapped packages and brilliant red poinsettias filled the space under and around the tree, while sparkling lights framed the entire scene.

"Something's not quite right," Kaylee murmured as she tilted her head.

"Talking to yourself again?" Mary set two steaming cups of cocoa on the counter beside the cash register. On this wintry Sunday afternoon, the two women were replacing the autumn displays with Christmas cheer at The Flower Patch, the florist shop Kaylee had purchased from her grandmother when she moved to Turtle Cove, Washington.

"I was talking to Bear."

Hearing his name, the dachshund barked, then sat up on his hind legs and pawed the air with his front feet. His bow tie, decorated with candy canes and peppermints, added to the festive mood.

"If only I knew what he was saying, then maybe I'd know what to do about this." Kaylee waved her hand at the display window. "The other window is beautiful. But this one . . . something seems off."

"Let me see," Mary offered. She took a moment to study Kaylee's arrangement, then disappeared into the workroom.

"Is it that bad?" Kaylee called after her.

"Not at all," Mary answered. She returned with a rectangular block which she deftly slid beneath the decorated pine tree and its draping.

"Ta-da!" she announced with a pleased smile. "The tree only needed more height."

Kaylee eyed the arrangement from different angles and gave a contented sigh. "Now it's perfect. What would I ever do without you?"

"You did most of the work. I just added a tiny tweak."

"That 'tiny tweak' made all the difference. Such a simple thing."

"Sometimes, maybe most of the time, the simplest thing is all that's needed."

"You're being very philosophical this afternoon."

"I'm just thinking about all the hoopla we allow ourselves to get involved with during the holidays," Mary said. "I'm still recovering from Thanksgiving dinner and the Black Friday shop-till-you-drop sales."

"You should be home taking it easy—"

"No place I'd rather be than right here," Mary interrupted. "This is where I always am the Sunday after Thanksgiving. Decorating The Flower Patch. It's tradition."

"I'm grateful for it."

"Besides, I wasn't really complaining. I love all the decorations and the lights and the presents." Mary's blue eyes twinkled behind her designer frames. "Especially the presents."

"But?" Kaylee prompted.

"But it might be nice, just for once, to have a simpler Christmas."

"I agree, but I don't think it will happen this year."

Mary chuckled. "It's your own fault that you got roped into the Festivity Committee's shenanigans. I warned you to stay away from Sylvia, but you didn't listen."

"It wasn't my fault," Kaylee protested. "She cornered me in the library. Smack dab between the biographies and the local history section. I really think she followed me there."

Sylvia Rosenthal and her sister owned The Chandlery Gift Shop across the street. That's what made it even stranger that the sixty-something widow had surprised Kaylee at the library. Her cheerful disposition had made it impossible to refuse her invitation—no, her insistence—that Kaylee join the committee.

"She may have," Mary said. "When Sylvia makes up her mind about something, nothing stops her. And she decided you were the perfect person to fill the vacant spot on the Festivity Committee."

"And so I did."

Not that Kaylee really minded. She wanted to participate in Turtle Cove's activities and traditions. When she'd first moved to Orcas Island, the Petal Pushers, her grandmother's gardening club, had welcomed Kaylee with open arms. Since then Kaylee had become acquainted with other local business owners, the town leaders, and her regular customers. She reveled in being part of such a close-knit community.

Mary's steady presence had also been a blessing. The retired police dispatcher, who kept her trim shape by taking tai chi classes, worked for Kaylee as a part-time floral designer.

No, not *for* Kaylee. Mary worked *with* Kaylee.

She meant what she'd said—Kaylee didn't know what she would do without Mary's good-natured practicality and talent for designing exceptional floral arrangements.

Mary and the other two Petal Pushers, Jessica Roberts, who owned the Death by Chocolate bakery next door, and DeeDee Wilcox, whose mystery bookstore was just down the street, were now Kaylee's dearest and closest friends in Turtle Cove.

"When's the next meeting?" Mary asked as she stirred her cocoa with a peppermint stick.

"Tuesday night. We're meeting at the Old Cape Lighthouse."

"But that's when the Petal Pushers meet."

"I told Sylvia, but it was the only time she could get all the committee members together." Kaylee peered into her cup, seemingly intent on its contents. "You know, we could use more help. The Petal Pushers could join us."

"Oh no." Mary practically guffawed. "We love you, Kaylee, but you will not sweet-talk us into that madness."

"Don't say no until you've heard me out."

Mary crossed her arms, but the stern expression on her face was softened by a faint smile. "I'm listening."

"I want to bring back the tree-lighting tradition." Kaylee's hopeful tone became more eager. "You know, the Petal Pushers and their families decorating a giant tree on the lawn at the Old Cape Lighthouse. Having the mayor turn on the lights. Cookies and cocoa. Candy canes. I loved that as a kid. It was always so fun."

"Do you know why they ended that tradition?"

"I asked Sylvia after the first meeting, but she just glared at me." Kaylee imitated Sylvia's Southern drawl. "'Darlin', we never, *never* speak of that debacle.'"

Mary laughed at Kaylee's impersonation. "Sylvia is right. We never do."

"You're not going to tell me?"

"Perhaps we should see how it looks from the street," Mary suggested. "In case we need to make any more tweaks."

"You're changing the subject."

"I know." Mary grabbed her coat and headed out the front door.

Given no other choice, Kaylee took a moment to plug in the strands of lights decorating both the front windows, shrugged into her heavy jacket, and joined Mary on the Victorian mansion's broad front porch.

She gazed at the windows as she stood beside the older woman. The lighted displays exuded a cheerful holiday spirit. Kaylee was pleased with their work, but she didn't want to say so until Mary had voiced her opinion.

Instead of saying anything, Mary descended the front steps and gazed back at the mansion from the middle of the quiet street. Most of the downtown shops were closed, though a few restaurants nearby were open. This was another Turtle Cove tradition Kaylee loved. The shop owners enthusiastically participated in the post-Thanksgiving shopping frenzy on Friday and Saturday. But this Sunday was a day of rest, the last one they'd have for a while as they catered to the holiday crowds.

Kaylee joined Mary in the street, lifting her face to the first snowflakes floating from the skies.

"Reese will be here tomorrow to put up the outside lights," Kaylee said. Kaylee and Reese Holt, the town's most sought-after handyman, had settled into an easygoing, comfortable friendship since Kaylee had come to live here.

"That will be like tying the bow on a vase," Mary said. "The perfect final touch."

The two women stood in silence for a few moments, both gazing at the historic Victorian with its many rooms and secrets. Kaylee supposed not even her grandmother, who had owned The Flower Patch for many years, knew all the mansion's nooks and crannies, nor all its mysteries.

The screech of brakes followed by the revving of a car engine broke the evening's peaceful tranquility. A bright red compact car on Shoreline Drive, the street that bordered the ocean, backed up, then turned onto Main Street.

Kaylee and Mary stepped onto the sidewalk as the vehicle came toward them. The driver slid to an abrupt stop and switched off the ignition.

"How strange," Mary said. "That's Gina Beckett. What in the world is she doing here?"

"I hope she's not complaining about her husband's flowers," Kaylee whispered, then forced a smile as an attractive brunette emerged from the car.

"Surely not," Mary whispered back then took a couple of steps forward. "Hi, Gina. What brings you downtown on a day like today?"

"I was on my way to Wildflower Cottage to see you." Gina's unflinching gaze bored into Kaylee, causing her to shift uncomfortably. "Then I just happened to glance down Main Street and there you were. Right in the street. It was a sign."

Kaylee inwardly groaned while her mind raced to think what Gina could have to complain about. The floral arrangements she and Mary had created for her husband's funeral were exactly what Gina had ordered—after changing her mind at least a dozen times.

Before Kaylee could speak, Mary gestured toward the mansion. "We were admiring the window displays."

Gina glanced at the windows then turned back to Kaylee without commenting on them. "I need to talk to you. It's very important."

"Perhaps I should be leaving," Mary said diplomatically.

"There's no need," Gina replied. "Maybe you can help too."

Kaylee and Mary exchanged curious glances, and Kaylee was even more certain Gina had a complaint.

"We'll help however we can," Kaylee said. "Let's go inside. We have a saucepan of cocoa on the stove."

"None for me," Gina said as they climbed the steps to the porch. "I'm glad I saw you. Saved me from driving all the way to your cottage."

"I'm glad too," Kaylee said. The only thing worse than handling a customer complaint was handling one in her home.

Fortunately, the majority of her customers loved their flowers and arrangements. She treated the few who didn't with as much grace and kindness as possible. Sometimes it seemed the unhappy customer only needed someone to listen. And after years of working with college students in her former life as a professor, Kaylee was skilled at listening. Still, complaints caused her neck muscles to tighten.

The women entered the shop, and Bear immediately greeted them with a bark and a fast-waving tail.

"Cute dog," Gina said perfunctorily.

"Thanks," Kaylee replied. "Why don't we go to the consultation area—I mean, the kitchen? We can talk in there."

The consultation area had the most comfortable seating, but large photographs of bridal bouquets lined the walls while cake toppers and other wedding items lined the shelves. It wasn't at all appropriate for meeting with a young woman whose husband had died only a week before.

"That's fine," Gina said. "Wherever you think best."

As soon as they were seated at the table, Gina pulled an envelope from her handbag. "I have something very important to show you. I hardly know what to think of it."

Curiosity replaced the dread in Kaylee's stomach. Maybe Gina wasn't here to complain after all. "What is it?" she asked.

"A note. A clue." Gina's wide-eyed gaze shifted between Kaylee and Mary. The uptight, terse persona disappeared as Gina transformed into someone with a bright and engaging personality.

"What kind of clue?" Kaylee asked.

"I don't know." Gina's voice trembled as if she were on the verge of tears, but her eyes gleamed with excitement. "That's why I brought it to you. I don't know what to make of it."

"To me?" Kaylee glanced again at Mary who shrugged subtly, clearly just as baffled as Kaylee.

"Who else? Everyone in town knows how great you are at solving mysteries. And this one has to be easy compared to some of the other cases you've been involved in."

"I'm not a detective," Kaylee hedged as she puzzled over Gina's odd demeanor. Self-assured one moment and choked with emotion the next, the young widow was a study in contradictions.

"This case will be fun," Gina said, brushing away Kaylee's protest. "Well, sad too. But there's no murder involved. I'd think you would be glad of that."

"Thrilled," Kaylee said flatly. Did Gina think she enjoyed solving murders? Gracious, no. They and other mysteries just seemed to come her way.

"Why don't you tell us about your note?" Mary said.

"I found it about an hour ago in Jake's boating office. You know, down at the marina. I was trying to find the checkbook, and I accidentally pulled the drawer out too far. But then the drawer wouldn't slide back in." Gina tapped the envelope. "This had fallen behind it."

"A note to Jake?" Kaylee asked.

"*From* Jake." Gina slid the envelope toward Kaylee. "See? It's addressed to me."

The printed lettering, written in a masculine hand, said: *To my only love.*

"Go ahead," Gina urged. "Open it."

Kaylee glanced at Mary then slid a card from the envelope. When she opened the card, a pressed sprig of lavender fell to the table, along with pressed lavender rose petals. The old-fashioned fragrance wafted upward, reminding Kaylee of long-ago summer mornings when she and her grandfather walked through the lavender fields behind the cottage.

"Isn't it romantic?" Gina said, her voice wavering. "Our

anniversary is next month. I'm sure he meant this as a surprise. Only now—" She stopped. "I still can't believe he's gone."

Mary placed a box of tissues on the table and squeezed Gina's arm. "I'm so sorry," she said. "You and Jake should have celebrated many more anniversaries together."

Kaylee hadn't met the Becketts before Jake's death, though she'd seen them around town a few times. But even she'd been shocked to learn that he had died of a heart attack. According to the obituary, he'd celebrated his twenty-sixth birthday only a couple of months ago.

"Read the note, Kaylee," Gina urged. "Please."

Kaylee cleared her throat and read the note aloud.

Let the adventure begin

Where vacations begin

For those not at home on the isle.

You know what to do to find the next clue.

These numbers reveal the smile.

48.597805, -122.943944

"What does it mean?" Kaylee asked.

"If I knew I wouldn't be here," Gina replied. "You have to help me figure it out, Kaylee. This is the last gift I have from Jake. If you don't help me—" Her voice caught and more tears gushed down her cheeks. "If you don't help me, I don't know what to do."

2

After giving Gina time to compose herself, Kaylee read the note out loud again.

Mary turned to Gina. "You must have some idea what he's talking about."

"But I don't. It's the best kind of mystery." Now that the tears were over, Gina was once again strangely upbeat. She shrugged out of her coat and propped her elbows on the kitchen table. "Where do vacations begin? At first, I thought maybe the marina. You know, with all the whale-watching tours and that kind of thing. But what does any of that have to do with a smile?"

"I can't imagine." Mary shifted her gaze to Kaylee. "Can you?"

"There's something about these numbers . . ." Kaylee pointed at the last line.

"Maybe they're a combination," Gina said. "Except Jake didn't have a safe, so I hope they aren't. A combination, I mean."

"It doesn't look like a phone number," Mary said.

"It's not. I tried dialing it, just in case. But I only got that recording. You know, 'Your call cannot be completed as dialed.'"

As the other two women talked, Kaylee concentrated on the spacing between the numbers. She'd seen numbers like these before.

"I know what they are," she said.

Mary and Gina stared at her.

"I used to date someone who was into satellite locations, things like that, when GPS was just getting started."

"These numbers are for a satellite?" Gina asked doubtfully. "What do satellites have to do with Orcas Island? Or with Jake?"

"They're a location," Kaylee said. "Longitude and latitude."

"I still don't get it," Gina replied.

"I do," Mary said. "It's a geocache."

"That's right." Kaylee pointed to the numbers again. "The first geocaching occurred near Portland, Oregon. This guy I used to date, he and I spent a lot of weekends tracking down locations. We even created a few of our own."

"Whatever happened to that guy?" Mary teased.

"He moved to Alaska to study weather patterns. I wasn't that keen on going with him."

Mary opened her mouth to say something, but Gina spoke before she could.

"Why would Jake leave me a geocache? We've never done anything like that before. I wouldn't even know how."

"It's not that hard. All you need is a geocache app. I'll show you." Kaylee pulled out her phone and searched for an appropriate app. Once it downloaded, she plugged in the numbers. A map of the southern shore of Orcas Island appeared on the screen. A red star marked the specific location.

Kaylee zoomed in on the star and smiled.

"There you have it, ladies. Where vacations begin for those who don't live here."

"Where?" Gina and Mary asked as they both tried to see the small screen in Kaylee's hand.

"The ferry landing."

Mary picked up the note. "It's easy once you know the answer, isn't it?"

"I still don't get it," Gina said. "Jake wanted me to go to the ferry landing? Why?"

"To find whatever he hid there," Kaylee said.

"I'm supposed to search the entire place? Why would he expect me to do that?"

"The numbers are more specific," Kaylee explained. "You

may have to search a bit, but you should be able to find the cache without too much trouble. Just download this app on your phone and follow the directions."

"You make it sound so easy." Gina's lips pressed into a pout as she rummaged through her bag. "He could have just written an address."

Kaylee and Mary exchanged glances. Mary patted Gina's hand. "I'm sure he meant well. He probably thought you'd enjoy a little mystery."

"Besides," Kaylee added, "addresses don't always work. The coordinates could be for, I don't know, a tree or maybe a lamppost. We found a cache buried beneath the slide at a school playground."

"I suppose you're right." Gina sounded doubtful but she held up her phone. "What's the app?"

Kaylee told her and Gina soon had the app installed on her phone. She entered the coordinates and the same map appeared on the screen.

"Guess I'll be driving to the ferry landing tomorrow. I just hope wherever he hid this thing won't be hard to find. I don't want to dig under a slide."

Kaylee ignored Gina's petulance and picked up the sprig of lavender. "Could this be a clue too?"

"And the part about a smile," Mary chimed in. "Perhaps that means something."

"Like what? Lavender grows all over this island. And who doesn't smile when they're on vacation?" Gina placed the sprig, petals, and card back into the envelope, shoved it into her bag, and stood. "Thanks for the help, Kaylee. At least now I know what those numbers mean."

"You're welcome." Kaylee led the way to the front of the shop while Gina put on her coat. "If you need anything else, just let me know."

"Do you mean that?"

Kaylee startled at the bluntness of the question. "Of course I mean it."

"Then come with me."

"What?"

"Come with me tomorrow. To the ferry." The pleading in Gina's eyes matched the tone of her voice. "You said you've done this kind of thing before. You'll know what to look for, where something could be hidden."

"I can't," Kaylee blurted, more because she was stunned at Gina's invitation than any other reason. Her mind scurried to soften the refusal. After all, Gina had just lost her husband. Her grief was almost palpable. But something more than grief seemed to have hold of Gina. Kaylee couldn't quite put her finger on it, but Gina was behaving—well, oddly. Her mood seemed to bounce between morose pouting and nervous energy. Driving to the ferry and back with her would be exhausting.

"There's so much to do here at the shop," she finally said. "This is one of our busiest times."

"I understand." Gina gazed around as if seeing the shop for the first time. "You have quite a successful business here, don't you?"

"We do all right."

"Jake had such dreams for his business. He built and repaired boats. It wasn't easy getting started, but he had some money saved. Enough to buy the business from the previous owner's widow, and he worked hard. I didn't much care for the long hours, but he promised we'd be rich someday. And then he died."

Pelted with guilt arrows, Kaylee didn't know what to say. She stood like a mannequin while Mary placed a motherly arm around Gina's shoulders.

"Jake was a go-getter, that's for sure," she said. "I'm sure he would have been a success."

"Thanks, Mary." Gina's eyes filled again. "I don't want to take up any more of your time, so I'll be going."

"Good luck tomorrow," Kaylee said. "I hope you find the cache."

"I hope so too. It'll be awfully sad if I don't."

Before Kaylee or Mary could say anything else, Gina was out the door and scurrying to her car.

"I feel so bad for her," Kaylee said. "And guilty."

"For not going with her?"

"You know me so well. But how can I? I've got appointments, orders, design work. Plus Christmas shopping and baking, and Reese is coming tomorrow. It's too much." Kaylee ended her mini tirade with a sigh. She did have a lot of items on her to-do list. But so did everyone else. Why was she making herself into a holiday martyr? "I'm sorry, Mary."

"No apologies needed. Though you do sound tired. I think we've done enough for one day, don't you?"

Before Kaylee answered, a knock sounded against the windowpane. Jessica Roberts's smiling face was practically pressed against the glass. Kaylee waved her in, and Jessica stamped her boots on the welcome mat.

"It's snowing," she announced.

"We know," Kaylee said. "What brings you by?"

"I got a new mystery from DeeDee's bookstore but left it at the bakery. I want to read it tonight."

"That's the advantage of an e-reader," Mary said. "You can access your library anytime from anywhere."

"Well, we have to support DeeDee," Jessica returned. "And call me old-fashioned, but I like a *real* book. Especially when it's signed by the author."

"You got Lorelei Lewis's latest?" Mary said then laughed. "Try saying that three times fast."

"No thanks. And yes, I did. DeeDee read an advance copy and said it's amazing. One of Lorelei's best."

"That's great," Kaylee said. "Sounds like things have worked out well for her." The first mystery Kaylee encountered after moving to Turtle Cove had indirectly involved the flamboyant author. And Kaylee's first wedding job had been for Lorelei's spoiled daughter and a guy nobody seemed to like except for his head-over-heels-in-love bride. It was hard to believe so much time had passed since then. From what Kaylee had heard through the Turtle Cove grapevine, Lorelei's daughter and son-in-law were blissfully happy.

"Your window displays are beautiful," Jessica said. "Mine are next, right?"

"You bet," Kaylee said. "As soon as you decide what theme you want. Will it be 'Chocolate Around the World' or 'Nutcracker's Enchanting Sweets'?"

"They both sound so fun and festive. You choose."

"Not going to happen," Kaylee said. "Your shop, your windows, your decision."

Jessica playfully groaned. "I'll let you know by noon tomorrow. Promise. I just saw Gina Beckett leaving. What was she doing here?"

"Curiosity . . ." Mary said in a lilting voice, leaving the rest of the phrase unspoken.

"That's why a cat has nine lives," Jessica retorted good-naturedly. "Curiosity kills it but can't keep it dead."

Kaylee laughed at her best friend's logic. "It's not a secret, really," she said. "Apparently Jake left Gina a note and she needed help deciphering it."

Jessica's eyes widened. "Like a code? Why did he do that?"

"She said it was probably an anniversary surprise."

"Did you figure it out?"

"Naturally," Mary said proudly. "Kaylee is Turtle Cove's Miss Marple, only younger and prettier. It took her maybe a minute."

"Thanks a lot, Mary," Kaylee said with a laugh.

"The note included numbers," Mary continued, "and Kaylee figured out they were a geocache location. To the ferry landing."

"He hid something for her there?" Jessica asked.

"Apparently."

"What fun!" Jessica exclaimed, then frowned. "Except, of course, that Jake is dead. Such a young man. It's really sad, isn't it?"

Kaylee and Mary murmured agreement.

"At least she'll be okay. Jake made sure Gina was protected."

"What do you mean?" Kaylee asked.

"The insurance policy," Jessica said offhandedly. "It's no surprise, really. Term insurance is cheap for young people, so they can get a substantial policy without spending a fortune."

"How substantial?" Kaylee held up her hand and shook her head. "Forget I asked. It's none of my business."

"Nor mine," Mary said. "But now I'm the curious cat."

"I don't really know," Jessica said. "Gina and her insurance agent were in the shop the other day talking, and she was signing papers. However much it was, I got the impression Gina was pleasantly surprised."

"The things people talk about in public." Mary tsked. "Private business should be discussed in private."

"What fun would that be?" Jessica asked in mock horror. "I think it must be an unwritten small-town rule. People say they don't want anyone else knowing their business, but there's nowhere they'd rather meet their accountants and lawyers and insurance agents than in a comfy bakery with good coffee and delicious pastries. Which is good business for me."

"And good for us too," Mary admitted. "I suppose it is the best way to be in the know on what's going on around here."

"I'm glad for her," Kaylee said. "Gina, I mean. That she'll be okay."

"But?" Mary asked.

"No 'but,'" Kaylee said. Though that wasn't quite true. The guilt of not agreeing to go with Gina was eating at her. Why did saying a simple *no* have to be so hard? Everything she had told Mary was true—her to-do list was long, her calendar swamped.

To distract her thoughts, she scooped Bear onto the counter and straightened his holiday bow tie. He licked her fingers, and she grinned and scratched behind his ears.

Mary glanced at the clock. "I need to go, but I'll be here bright and early in the morning."

"Thanks for all your help," Kaylee said. "I couldn't have done it without you."

"I know." Mary gave her a tender smile. "Your grandmother used to say the same."

"I'll get going too." Jessica headed toward the door, then stopped and turned back to Kaylee. "The music from *The Nutcracker* is going around and around in my head. There. I made the decision."

"So you definitely want the 'Nutcracker's Enchanting Sweets' theme?" Kaylee asked.

"Definitely," Jessica said, though doubt weakened her tone.

"You're sure?"

Jessica groaned and covered her face. "I don't know!"

Kaylee shook her head with a grin. "Oh, Jess. How about if we do the Nutcracker theme for Christmas and the Around the World theme for Valentine's Day? Then you can have both."

"Do they celebrate Valentine's Day around the world?" Jessica asked.

"If they don't, they should."

"I like it." Jessica gripped the door handle. "It's decided. Thanks, Kaylee."

She opened the door and, after a final wave, closed it behind her.

"Finally," Mary said. "I didn't think she was ever going to choose."

"At least we guessed right," Kaylee said as she reached under the counter for Bear's winter coat. "Don't you ever tell her I already ordered the nutcracker soldiers."

"My lips are sealed." Mary put on her coat and wrapped a long scarf around her neck. "You ready to go?"

"As soon as I do a quick walk-through. I want to make sure everything is ready for tomorrow. But you go ahead."

"I don't mind waiting."

"No need, but thanks."

After Mary left, Kaylee washed their mugs, then checked the calendar and the order sheet for the next day. After she fastened Bear's coat around his chest, she locked the front door and turned out the lights in the windows. As darkness descended on the shop and she headed out the back door, an unsettled feeling descended on Kaylee.

She couldn't get the image of Gina's pleading gaze out of her mind. But really, how could she possibly take time to go to the ferry? Gina could do this on her own. She *should* do it on her own. Or she could ask one of her friends to go with her.

This wasn't Kaylee's problem.

So why did she feel like it was?

3

Kaylee tossed the magazine she'd been browsing onto the kitchen island at Wildflower Cottage, her home, and lit a lavender-scented candle. She smiled as she breathed in the subtle fragrance and was transported once again to her childhood visits. When she and Grandpa Ed wandered through the lavender fields behind the cottage, gathering blossoms for Grandma's glass vases, his eyes would sparkle with mischief as he told Kaylee tall tales of his youthful adventures at sea.

Most of the stories weren't true, and her grandmother, Bea, had often chided her husband for filling Kaylee's head with nonsense. But then Grandpa and Kaylee would exchange winks when Grandma wasn't looking. Even at her young age, Kaylee understood that it didn't matter whether the stories were embellished. She was making memories with Grandpa to hide in her heart.

No one could take those precious gifts away from her.

Kaylee filled the kettle with water, then opened her refrigerator door and stared at the contents. She and Kathy Fitz, the head librarian of the Orcas Island Library, had met at The Ideal Meal after church for a scrumptious seafood buffet dinner. Kaylee always enjoyed getting together with Kathy. And the seafood had been a nice change after living on Thanksgiving leftovers for the past couple of days.

But she didn't want seafood again today, so she had a late supper of grilled cheese and tomato soup. After lighting a fire in the living room fireplace, she scooped Bear into her arms and carried him to the room that had once been her grandfather's study. A bookshelf he had made from barnwood stood against one wall, lined with all the mystery novels he'd amassed during his lifetime. Kaylee loved the way the room kept her grandfather alive in her heart.

"What do you say, Bear? This is a good night for one of Grandpa's mysteries, don't you think? One of the classics."

He yipped, which she could only interpret as agreement. She chose a favorite Agatha Christie she had read as a teen and ambled back into the living room to curl up in front of the fire. Bear snuggled beside her, pushing his long nose beneath her leg.

Kaylee tried to read a page or two, then gave up. None of the words were sticking in her head. Instead, her mind kept replaying Gina's visit to The Flower Patch. For reasons Kaylee couldn't quite understand, she just couldn't get a handle on the young woman. It had started with their initial meeting, when Gina had come into the shop to talk about flowers for her husband's funeral.

Kaylee's heart had gone out to the young widow, and she'd excused Gina's odd combination of flightiness and bluster. After all, the young woman was grieving the death of the man she had expected to grow old with. The Becketts had only been married a couple of years, and Gina was still in her early twenties. Her parents had moved to California shortly after Gina's marriage. They came back for the funeral but hadn't stayed long.

Her brother, Chad, had supported her through the ordeal, but Kaylee wasn't sure what to make of him either. He'd been polite, even helpful when it came to positioning the various flower arrangements throughout the church. But he exuded a strange kind of nervous energy as if electrical currents jolted along his limbs.

Amused by the image, Kaylee chuckled. "I'm getting fanciful," she said to Bear, who responded by burrowing further beneath her leg. She shifted to give him space. "Or maybe I'm feeling guilty."

Had she really become so preoccupied with her own concerns that she couldn't spend an hour or two helping someone else? *You're not acting in the spirit of the season,* she scolded herself.

The doorbell rang. Startled by the sound, Kaylee practically dropped her novel. Bear barked as he jumped from the love seat and raced toward the front door.

Kaylee followed him as the bell rang again. She opened the door.

Reese stood on the front porch, an amicable grin on his face and a covered dish in his hands. As usual, his brown hair needed a trim and stubble darkened his jawline.

"Come in," Kaylee said, shivering at the blast of wind that swept through the open doorway. "What brings you here?"

"I was needed in the neighborhood, so I thought I'd stop by." He kicked the snow off his boots and handed Kaylee the dish. Inside the foyer, he greeted Bear with a quick tummy rub, then removed his boots and jacket.

"Who needed you?" she asked.

"The Camerons. I keep telling them to replace their old water heater fittings, but they don't want to. So I add a bit more plumber's tape and cross my fingers."

"If you weren't so good with that tape, maybe they wouldn't have a choice."

"You've got a point." He brushed melting snow from his hair. "That dish is courtesy of Mrs. Cameron by the way."

"Her apple pandowdy?"

"Straight out of the oven."

"To the kitchen. Fast."

Reese sat down at the island while Kaylee retrieved forks and napkins. Reese uncovered the casserole dish and inhaled the delicious aroma of baked apples and cinnamon. Kaylee speared an apple slice with her fork and savored the first bite.

"Mmmm, that's good. I'll get plates."

"Don't bother." Reese stuck his fork in the opposite end. "No one makes pandowdy like Lizzie Cameron, and there's no better way to eat it than straight out of the dish."

"You're right." Kaylee took another bite. "I tried making this once, but mine didn't turn out nearly this good. Do you think she has a secret ingredient?"

"I know her secret ingredient. But I'll never tell, so don't bother asking."

"What if I guess? You could at least give me a hint."

"Quit your badgering or I'll take my pandowdy and go home."

"Rude." Kaylee grabbed the dish and pulled it closer to her side of the island.

Reese tugged it back and shoveled a large forkful of the dessert into his mouth.

Kaylee laughed and took her own huge bite.

After he swallowed, Reese hummed with contentment. "Glad you and Bear didn't mind me barging in on you."

"I'm glad you did. We weren't really doing anything. Mary and I decorated the windows at The Flower Patch so we're all ready for Christmas."

"Except for the outdoor lights. I'll be there bright and early in the morning to take care of them. Expect me five minutes before Jess opens the bakery. I need to get my morning cup of coffee first. And an egg-and-bacon sandwich."

"Wait a minute. Don't you mean five minutes *after* Jess opens?"

"Nah," he said in an affected drawl. "I've got special privileges. When I have to get an early start to the day, Jess helps me out with breakfast."

"If you're too busy tomorrow, the lights can wait a day or two."

"I'd rather get them done. Besides, I promised. It's just that a few extra jobs came up. Always that way this time of year."

"I know what you mean. I feel a little slammed myself with all the holiday orders to fill and centerpieces to be designed. Not that I'm complaining. I love the work."

"Me too. Though it might be fun to trade places for a day. I'll hang around The Flower Patch and you can sweet-talk the Camerons into buying new water heater fittings."

They both laughed. Reese's warm voice and teasing banter were like a breath of fresh air, just what she needed right now. Without realizing it, she exuded a heavy sigh.

Immediately she wished she could take it back and hoped Reese hadn't noticed. A vain hope.

"Something wrong?"

"Not really."

"That's not too convincing."

Kaylee hesitated a moment. Gina might not want anyone else to know about the card her husband had left for her. On the other hand, she hadn't said anything about keeping it a secret.

She stared out the kitchen window. Night enveloped the cottage, and it was impossible to see the snow. But somehow she knew it still fell, silent and lovely upon the frozen ground. Like the snow, the afternoon's events once again swirled in her mind.

"Do you know Gina Beckett?"

"Sure. I did odd jobs for Jake sometimes. Why?"

"She stopped by The Flower Patch when Mary and I were there."

"And?"

Kaylee's natural reticence won out. She wouldn't tell Reese about the card and the geocache. At least not yet.

"She asked me to go to the ferry landing with her as a favor."

"And you said no and now you feel guilty about it."

"You don't pull any punches, do you, Mr. Holt?"

"Hey, I've been in those boots. But you're busy, right? All these orders and centerpieces."

"That's not even the half of it. Sylvia Rosenthal shanghaied me too. Now I'm on the Festivity Committee on top of everything else."

Reese gave a hearty laugh. "You gotta love Sylvia."

"Maybe *you* do," Kaylee retorted with a wry smile. "Actually, I don't mind. It'll be fun, but there are only so many hours in a day."

"You said no, Kaylee. There's nothing wrong with that."

"Then why do I feel so bad?"

"Because you have a tender heart. You know Gina is grieving." He toyed with an apple slice smothered in cinnamon sauce, his mood uncharacteristically serious. "I remember when her boyfriend died when they were teenagers. She took it really hard. And now to lose her husband? That's a lot for anyone to go through."

Kaylee frowned as she caught his gaze. "Her boyfriend died?"

"Must have been four, maybe five years ago."

"What happened?"

"I don't think anyone really knows. Roz Corzo found him in his skiff just drifting out in West Sound. Fortunately she didn't have a boatload of tourists with her at the time."

Roz, the gruff owner of Corzo Whale Watch, had once given Kaylee a much-needed clue when she had investigated her grandfather's disappearance. Roz had noticed one of those small details no one else had seen. Kaylee was certain that not much escaped the woman's eagle eye.

From there Kaylee's imagination ran wild. What were the chances that Gina's boyfriend and husband had both died? Was the young woman a black widow in disguise?

"I know what you're thinking," Reese said.

"I don't think you do."

"Gina didn't kill her boyfriend. And she definitely didn't kill Jake. He died because of his heart, remember? Don't be looking for mysteries where there aren't any, Kaylee."

"They seem to come looking for me."

Reese chuckled. "They sure do. People on the mainland think of us as living in a quiet little backwater town where nothing exciting ever happens. If only they knew."

"Every small town has its secrets."

"And its colorful characters."

"Who are you thinking of, specifically?"

"We've already mentioned two of them. Roz Corzo and—"

"Sylvia Rosenthal." They said her name at the same time and laughed.

Kaylee took one last cinnamony bite, then placed her fork in the sink. This was the life she'd dreamed of during long and unproductive faculty meetings at the university—a quiet evening in a cozy kitchen enjoying good food and the easy banter of a close friend. She couldn't have asked for a more perfect ending to what had been a mostly pleasant day. The only real upset had been Gina's appearance at The Flower Patch.

What was Gina doing this evening?

Kaylee envisioned the young woman curled in a tight ball in the corner of a couch, her body wracked with sobs and mascara running down her pale cheeks. The image caught at Kaylee's heart.

"When will your parents get here?" Reese's question broke into her thoughts.

"They aren't coming."

"I thought it was all settled."

"It was. But things changed." Kaylee's parents hadn't been back to Turtle Cove since their move to Florida several years ago. Both were now retired and lived only a mile or two from Kaylee's brother, Kyle, and his family.

After several weeks of calls and e-mails, all the plans had been made for an extended road trip from the southeast corner of the United States to the northwest corner. The Bleus were shopping for an RV which they planned to drive to Arizona to visit Kaylee's grandmother and her twin sister. After that, they'd head to California and up the coastal highway to Orcas Island.

"What happened?" Reese asked, concern showing on his face.

"Why don't we go sit by the fireplace? It's a bit chilly in here."

Once they settled in the living room, Kaylee and Bear on the love seat and Reese in the matching chair, he asked his question again.

"Dad got a temporary job," Kaylee replied.

"I thought he was retired."

"He's supposed to be. But this opportunity came up and apparently it was too good not to take it."

"He's a mechanical engineer, right?"

"Yes, but this position has something to do with reviewing potential patents. Anyway, the pay will boost their savings, so they've promised to do the whole RV thing next summer." Kaylee pulled an afghan tighter around her legs, and Bear burrowed beneath the folds. "So I'll just have to wait a few more months to see them."

She tried to put a bright note in her voice, but it sounded false even to her own ears. No way Reese would be fooled into thinking she was okay with this.

"Are you going to them?"

"I checked into it, but I've waited too long to get a good price on a flight." She turned to him and smiled. "I was disappointed when they first told me. It seems forever since we've had a Christmas together. But I know it's hard for Mom to leave the grandkids on a holiday. Besides, things always seem to have a way of working out for the best."

"Maybe not always, but I'd say usually," he said dubiously.

"What about you? Any plans?"

"Same as always. Driving down to Los Angeles to be with the family."

"That's good," Kaylee said lamely, feeling a tiny bit sorry for herself. She didn't mind so much that her parents lived close to their grandchildren. But why did they have to live at the other end of the country? Reese might have a long drive to visit his family, but at least they lived on the same coast.

The minutes slowly passed with long silences, companionable rather than awkward, separating their occasional conversation. When Kaylee's phone rang, it startled both of them.

"It's Mary," she said. "Do you mind?"

"Of course not," Reese said.

She nodded then answered the call while walking into the kitchen. Bear followed close at her heels.

"Hi, Mary. Everything okay?"

"I've just been thinking."

"About what?"

"You and Gina."

"She's been on my mind too."

"Are you going with her to the ferry?"

"I don't see how I can."

Mary hesitated a moment before speaking, but Kaylee could hear volumes in that momentary silence.

"Sometimes you just have to *do*," Mary finally said. "I'll come in early to get started on the orders and on Jessica's window arrangements. I promise you'll be glad you went with her."

"You're probably right. I'll call her now."

"You didn't take much persuading."

"I've just been thinking about how hard this Christmas is going to be for her. How lonely."

"Lonely for you too?"

"I wish my parents hadn't changed their plans." It was the first time she'd said the words out loud, and she felt like a child saying them to Mary. But the older woman's comfort and affection seemed to zip right through the air and wrap Kaylee into a hug.

"I know. But you know you're welcome to join Herb and me. There'll be lots of food and games."

"I'll think about it. Thank you."

"Think about going to the ferry landing or think about coming over for Christmas dinner?"

"The latter. I've already decided about the ferry."

After ending the call, Kaylee returned to the living room to find Reese poking at the fire.

"I'd better be going," he said as he stood and returned the poker to its stand. "But I'll see you in the morning. Early."

Kaylee let Bear out and walked outside with Reese, hugging herself against the cold, then waved as he drove away. Bear's short legs carried him surprisingly quickly back into the warmth of the cottage.

She returned to the fireplace and perched on the hearth while staring at her phone's display screen. She made a point of placing her customers' information in her contact list, so she had Gina's number.

Mary hadn't said everything she was thinking. The older woman knew without being told that Kaylee was in the dumps because of her parents' change of plans. Normally, Kaylee would never have hesitated to say yes to a request like Gina's.

She needed to make this right.

She quickly found the number and hit the send button. The call went to voice mail.

"Hi, Gina. This is Kaylee Bleu. I'd like to go with you to the ferry landing tomorrow. If you still want me to. If so, just give me a call. I'll be up a bit longer."

After disconnecting the call, she smiled at Bear. "Mary was right. I feel better already."

Kaylee had barely finished her sentence when the phone rang.

"Do you mean it?" Gina asked without any preamble or pretense of a greeting. Her voice sounded shaky, as if she had been crying.

No, Kaylee quickly realized. *She's still crying.* "Yes."

"Is nine too early?"

"Not at all. I'll pick you up at your house."

"I can drive."

Kaylee bit the inside of her cheek. If Gina got distraught, Kaylee didn't want her behind the wheel. "I really don't mind."

"Okay," Gina said, and her voice sounded a little less weepy. "But I'll come to The Flower Patch. We can leave from there."

"Great. I'll see you in the morning."

"It'll be fun, you'll see." Gina's voice caught. "Or maybe not."

If Kaylee was a betting person, she'd have placed money on the latter. A strange chill ran up her spine.

Doing the right thing was the right thing to do. So where did this sense of foreboding come from?

4

Blinking against the morning sunlight, Kaylee handed the string of lights to Reese. He towered above her, balancing on the ladder on a step too high for Kaylee's comfort. "Are you sure that's safe?" she fussed as he leaned to the left to loop a strand over the next hook.

"Are you sure you're not Nervous Nellie pretending to be my friend Kaylee?" he teased. "I've been doing this for years. I'm not going to fall."

"Famous last words."

"Don't jinx me with your portents of doom." He straightened, resting his weight against the ladder while he unwound another section of the lights.

"'Portents of doom'?"

"How about 'omens of disaster'?"

"How about you watch what you're doing instead of making up ominous phrases?"

"Only if you stop worrying so much. I know my limits."

Again, famous last words.

Kaylee refrained from saying what she was thinking. He was definitely more of a risk-taker than she was, especially when it came to climbing ladders and stretching too far on one side or the other. She glanced at her watch. Gina would be arriving soon, and Reese still had another section to complete.

"I'll try not to worry," she said. "But you have to promise you won't get on the ladder if no one is out here with you."

"That's not a problem. I'll just grab someone from the bakery to stand guard."

"What if no one's there?"

"Then I'll get someone from the diner. Don't be such a fussbudget."

His tone sounded off, as if he were hiding actual annoyance. Kaylee took a small step back. She wasn't being a fussbudget or a worrywart or a Nervous Nellie or anything else he might decide to call her, but Reese seemed a bit out of sorts. Perhaps, like her, he was feeling overwhelmed with his holiday to-do list.

"When did you say Gina was coming?" Reese's voice had resumed its usual good-natured tone, though it sounded a little forced. He must have realized he'd been a tad on the grumpy side.

Kaylee decided to let the issue pass. It wasn't worth thinking about, not when she knew Reese was seldom short with anyone.

"In about five minutes," she said.

Reese concentrated on stringing the lights on the other side of the ladder, again reaching as far as he could to hook the wires. Kaylee kept a hand on the ladder's leg and tried not to imagine the ladder and Reese falling into the hedge.

When he got the section situated to his liking, he climbed down, then stood back to inspect his work. He smiled at Kaylee. "See? Back on terra firma with nary a scratch."

"Who says 'nary' anymore? And the job isn't finished yet."

"It will be before you get back from the ferry landing. Unless you're planning to drive there, turn right around, and drive back."

"We'll be gone longer than that." For the umpteenth time, she almost told him about the cache. She had slept fitfully, her dreams a mixture of worry and disappointment. Even with the GPS coordinates, they might have trouble finding the cache. And what if someone else had already stumbled across it? There might not be anything to find.

A vehicle pulled to the curb and Kaylee turned toward the sound, expecting to see Gina. Instead a rusted pickup with a dented fender belched black smoke before the engine stopped knocking. A thin young man slowly emerged from the driver's side. Kaylee immediately recognized him from the funeral.

Chad Sinclair, Gina's older brother.

He pushed thick locks of dark hair from his forehead, and Kaylee immediately noticed the fading bruise on his jaw. It had been more noticeable at the funeral. She and Jessica had speculated about what might have happened—it rather looked like someone had punched him—but not even Jessica, with all her snooping and eavesdropping skills, had discovered who had delivered the blow.

That hadn't stopped Jessica from deciding she knew what had happened. Always up for a good conspiracy story, she was convinced that Chad had somehow gotten mixed up with modern-day pirates. Her tale grew more outlandish each time she told it until Chad, who had the intimidation factor of a gnat, was as dangerous as Blackbeard.

Kaylee's theory was much less thrilling. A simple brawl, perhaps over a girl or a sports event or perhaps for no reason at all, had resulted in Chad sporting the purple—now greenish-yellow—souvenir.

He loped toward Reese and Kaylee, his hands shoved deep into the pockets of his heavy coat and his shoulders hunched against the cold.

"Kaylee. Reese," he said, acknowledging each with a nod.

"Hey, Chad," Reese replied.

"I thought my sister might be here."

"I'm expecting her at any moment," Kaylee said.

Chad focused his attention on Kaylee. "She told me you're driving her to the ferry landing."

"That's right."

"I know you mean well, but do you really think that's a good idea?"

"Why wouldn't it be?"

"Just seems like a silly goose chase to me. She's still grieving over Jake, grieving hard. Why go poking in a fresh wound?"

Kaylee exchanged a quick glance with Reese, who raised one eyebrow in a puzzled gesture. Now she definitely wished she had told him the entire story.

"Gina asked me to take her, and I promised I would," Kaylee said. "Maybe it's what she needs to do to help ease her grief."

"Begging your pardon, but I don't think you know my sister as well as I do."

Reese stiffened at Chad's tone. "Now wait a minute—"

"It's okay," Kaylee said, placing her hand on Reese's arm. "Chad. I would never presume such a thing. Gina and I are practically strangers, but—"

"Then why did she come to you with that crazy note?"

"What note?" Reese asked.

Kaylee decided she could explain everything to Reese later. Right now, she needed to figure out why Chad was so upset with her.

"She thought I could help," Kaylee said. "And I did."

"You really think Jake hid something near the ferry? That he expected Gina to know what those numbers meant and go looking for it?"

Maybe she shouldn't have agreed to go with Gina. But how could she have known Chad would make such a big deal out of a simple trip?

"I really don't know what Jake did or didn't do, or what he expected Gina to know or not know." Kaylee tried to keep the frustration out of her voice, but it seeped in anyway. "But Gina asked for my help and she asked me to go with her. And that's exactly what I'm going to do."

Chad lowered his gaze to his boots and scuffed at the snow.

Early this morning, before Reese had set up the ladder, the snow had been beautifully white and pristine. But now it was slushy and gray. Both Kaylee's and Reese's boots had crunched through the thin top layer. By afternoon, most of the snow would probably have melted away.

In a way, Kaylee felt like her good intentions had been squashed too. Not by Chad's boots, but by his frosty demeanor.

He raised his head and opened his mouth, but before he could say anything, Gina appeared.

"Hey, everyone," she said in a singsong voice, then stopped in surprise at seeing her brother. "Chad. What are you doing here?"

"Just wanted to talk to Kaylee."

"I tried to call you," Gina said to her brother as she neared the group. "Strangest thing. My car wouldn't start this morning."

"How did you get here then?" Chad asked.

"Mr. Riley from next door dropped me off. He was on his way to the pier, but he said he didn't mind taking the long way around because it gave him an excuse to stop in at the bakery for a cup of coffee, a donut, and the morning gossip."

The longer Gina talked, the more annoyed Chad seemed to get. But she seemed oblivious to his growing frustration.

"Can you go over later and see what's wrong? It worked fine yesterday."

"Maybe on my lunch hour."

"Great." Gina faced Kaylee with a bright smile on her face. "Good thing you're driving instead of me, isn't it? It's a long walk to the ferry. Are you ready to go?"

"I need to get my keys," Kaylee said, then poked Reese. "Promise you'll get someone to hold the ladder."

"I promise," he said. His expression darkened as he glanced at Chad. "Time for a bit of a break anyway."

He closed the ladder and leaned it against the outer wall of the mansion. "Hey, Chad, want to join me for a cup of coffee? My treat."

Chad bit at his lip and shook his head. "Got things to do, man. Another time."

"Sure," Reese said. He kept his gaze on Chad, who scuffed at the snow again, shoulders hunched.

"You won't forget to check out my car, will you?" Gina called after him as he walked toward his pickup.

Instead of answering, he waved in acknowledgement.

Gina shivered within her coat, but her smile remained radiant. This morning she definitely wasn't the picture of a grieving widow. Instead she had the appearance of a young woman eager for an adventure.

"I'll be back out in a minute or two." Kaylee headed inside as Reese asked Gina about her car. She didn't catch Gina's reply, but her tone was breezy and carefree. She didn't seem too concerned, but then with a mechanic as a brother, perhaps a nonworking car wasn't a big deal.

When Kaylee reached the porch, she glanced down the street. Chad's beat-up truck disappeared around the corner, belching black smoke behind it as he turned on to Shoreline Drive.

A case of the shoemaker's children not having any shoes, Kaylee mused, though she doubted Chad would have appreciated the comparison.

Gina's laughter floated through the crisp winter air as Kaylee entered the mansion. She paused a moment, disturbed by the sound without knowing why. Both Gina and her brother seemed a little weird. And not in that small-town "colorful character" kind of way. That phrase described people like Sylvia Rosenthal and Roz Corzo. The two women might be a bit odd and set in their ways, but they weren't . . . Kaylee searched her mind for the appropriate word and came up with two: *socially awkward.*

That's all it was. The Sinclair siblings lacked competent social skills. So Gina bounced from despondency to euphoria and back again while Chad glowered and shuffled his feet.

Though perhaps Kaylee wasn't being fair. Gina's loss was still new, and perhaps Chad had been close to his brother-in-law. He hadn't openly grieved during the funeral, but he'd certainly been a rock for Gina. He'd probably buried his own feelings to provide emotional support for her.

If that was the case, maybe that's all he was trying to do now. As Kaylee dug her keys from her bag, the strange conversation with Chad replayed itself in her mind. This time, instead of seeing him as socially inept, she thought of him as a protective brother, Gina's only family member in Turtle Cove. No one could blame him for being worried about his sister.

Kaylee just wished she could have told him that she wasn't gung ho about this drive either.

But it no longer mattered. She had made a promise and Gina was waiting.

She only hoped they could find Jake's hidden cache without Gina suffering a meltdown.

5

Thankfully, the short drive to the ferry landing was much quieter than Kaylee had anticipated. Before they left, she put Jake's GPS coordinates in her navigation app so she'd know exactly where to go. As they drove south on Orcas Road, Gina leaned her head against the passenger side window, her focus seemingly intent on the blanketed landscape. Traffic was light, and the road crews had already cleared the highway of the night's snowfall. The sun's rays, pale against the gray backdrop of the sky, still managed to glisten.

As they drew closer to the landing, Kaylee's navigation app came to life, the accented voice providing direction, then announcing that the destination was on her right. She pulled into the parking lot of a picturesque strip mall anchored by a gift shop and café. The architecture was reminiscent of an old-fashioned whaling village but with all the modern conveniences.

Kaylee parked her SUV in an empty space near the café.

"Now what?" Gina asked without enthusiasm, her gaze still intent on the passenger window.

"We don't have to do this, you know," Kaylee said softly. "Maybe Chad is right, and this isn't such a good idea."

Gina harrumphed. "Chad hasn't been right about anything ever. Not in his whole life."

"I doubt that's true."

"How would you know?" Her tone was childish and petty. Without even seeing her face, Kaylee knew Gina's mouth was tucked into a pout.

"Because he had to make several decisions on the day of Jake's funeral. Nothing earth-shattering or major. But still important. And he made those decisions so you didn't have to be bothered with them. Good decisions."

"Like what?"

"One of the pallbearers canceled at the last minute and Chad found a replacement. Did you know that?"

Gina shook her head.

"Other things too. Like I said, nothing major, yet they still needed doing."

They sat in silence for a few moments then Gina quoted a portion of Jake's note from memory. "'You know what to do to find the next clue. These numbers reveal the smile.'" She faced Kaylee. "What do you suppose it means? To find the *next* clue. Why did Jake do this?"

The words settled into Kaylee's brain, and she let out a slow breath. She'd been so intent on the numbers and what they meant she hadn't paid much attention to the rest of the note. "Did he like puzzles?"

"Not that I ever knew. What if he made even more clues, and this is only the first?"

Kaylee shook her head. *Please let this be the only one.* She had too many things to do to be playing this game all day. Instead of one geocaching adventure, this appeared to be turning into some type of scavenger hunt.

But she didn't want her own frustration to affect Gina's already fragile state.

She switched off the ignition and smiled brightly. "We're not going to know until we find the first cache. Let's do this."

Gina's lips gradually turned upward, and her eyes sparkled with growing excitement. "We're the two musketeers."

She hopped out of the SUV, glanced around the parking lot, then peered over the hood at Kaylee.

"Make that the three musketeers," she said as she pointed to a dented pickup parked a few spaces away. "Chad's here."

Kaylee hit the remote to lock her vehicle while Gina scampered to Chad and threw her arms around his neck in a sisterly hug made awkward by the heaviness of their coats. For a moment, Kaylee thought they were both going to end up on the pavement as Gina's exuberance almost caused Chad to lose his balance. But they managed to stay upright.

"Hi, Kaylee." Chad's demeanor was completely different than it had been less than half an hour ago at The Flower Patch.

"Hi, Chad. I'm surprised to see you," Kaylee said.

He blushed slightly. "Gina was so determined that I figured I might as well help her out. Not that I have any idea what that clue means."

"I'm glad you came," Kaylee said.

"Isn't this fun?" Gina exclaimed. Her earlier moodiness seemed to have melted away. She pulled Jake's note from her pocket and pointed to the numbers. "We need to find this place."

"I already have them plugged in," Kaylee said. She opened the geocache app and studied the small dot, then scanned the parking lot to get her bearings. "What did the note say about the numbers?"

"'These numbers reveal the smile,'" Gina recited from memory.

"Look over there." Kaylee pointed beyond Gina to the sign of a small storefront tucked on the other side of the café. Gina and Chad both pivoted to see for themselves. "I think we found it."

The golden sign of a beachwear boutique depicted a smiling sun.

"That was easy." Gina clapped her mittened hands, seeming almost giddy.

"We haven't found the cache yet," Kaylee cautioned.

"But we will," Gina replied. "I just know it."

The three headed for the store, but stopped at the closed door. A placard on the window said the boutique was closed for the winter.

"Can they do that?" Gina asked. "I mean, how can anyone have a store so close to the ferry that's not open all year round?"

"No idea," Chad said with a shrug. "But if Jake put a geocache here it has to be accessible."

"I would think so." Kaylee scrutinized the store's exterior. "Where would I hide a geocache?" she murmured, more to herself than to Gina and Chad. She peered at the eaves. "Not too high up because that would make it hard to retrieve. But he wouldn't have wanted anyone to find it by accident either."

"Do you think he buried it?" Chad asked as he frowned doubtfully at the semi-frozen ground between the parking lot and the storefront. "That wouldn't have been easy."

"We're just going to have to search for anything that seems out of place," Kaylee said. "Chad, you might want to look up into the trees if you can. I found a geocache once that was disguised with pine branches and pinecones."

"I'm on it." He immediately examined the nearest evergreen.

"What about me?" Gina asked. "What can I do?"

"Let's make our way around to the back," Kaylee suggested. "It's less likely someone would have accidentally stumbled on something hidden at the rear of the store."

"Good idea."

The two women walked past several storefronts before finding a narrow passageway that allowed access to the rear of the stores. The adjoining alley, bordered on one side by a stockade fence and the other by the buildings, was barely large enough for two vehicles to pass each other. Dumpsters and other bulky items lined the brick wall.

"A loose brick?" Gina asked doubtfully.

"That'd be hard to find," Kaylee said. "But it's not going to be around any of these Dumpsters. Too risky. It might have gotten thrown away."

"Where then?"

"I don't know." Kaylee scanned the area, again asking herself where she would hide a geocache intended for only one person. Where was the best place to hide something and be sure no one else found it?

"Read the clue again," Kaylee said.

"I don't have to read it. I memorized it. Except for the numbers. 'Let the adventure begin where vacations begin for those not at home on the isle.'"

"That's it," Kaylee said. "'Home on the isle.'" She pointed to an area beside the rear door of the boutique. "Somebody carved a drawing into that brick."

The carving, though rustic and worn, definitely resembled a simple house next to a mound with a palm tree on it, like a cartoon representing a deserted island.

"It looks like a child's drawing," Gina said.

"Was Jake artistic?"

"He sketched out the dock assignments for boats at the marina, things like that. But nothing fancy."

"I don't suppose it was easy to etch into the brick. Why don't you see if it's loose?"

Gina took off her mittens and tried to get a grip on the brick. "I don't think it is."

"We need a tool."

"Chad probably has something in his truck."

It was a good suggestion. A logical one, even. But for a reason she couldn't explain, Kaylee preferred to keep Chad's involvement to a minimum. He'd been so adamant that she not encourage Gina—and she definitely hadn't—but now he was as supportive as any brother could ever be. Which version of Chad was the genuine one?

Kaylee had no way of knowing.

"Let me try to loosen it." Kaylee searched the ground and found a narrow piece of rock nearby. She ran the edge of the rock along the mortar on the top of the brick, and the brick seemed to shift. "I think it's working. And I don't think this is mortar."

"Then what is it?"

"Not sure." Kaylee pressed her finger into the substance. "It's rubbery and removes easily. I think it's some kind of caulk."

She finished scraping along the edges of the brick, then stepped back and gestured to Gina. This was her cache—she should be the one to finish the job.

Gina managed to grasp the top and bottom edges of the brick. After a couple of tries, the brick slid out and she gasped in delight.

"We did it!"

"Did what?" Chad hurried toward them. "You actually found it?" Disbelief lowered his tone, and he seemed on edge.

"Here." Gina thrust the brick into his hands and bent to peer into the cavity. "I think I see something."

She straightened with a glance at Kaylee. But instead of saying anything, she only took a deep breath as if bracing herself for whatever she might find in the cache. A wave of sympathy washed over Kaylee. She'd been so caught up in solving the clue and finding the cache that she'd temporarily forgotten how emotional this moment would be for Gina.

Kaylee gave Gina an encouraging smile and gently squeezed her arm. She glanced at Chad, but he stared at the dark hole in the brick wall. His expression was sullen, almost wary.

Was he afraid of what Gina was going to find?

Don't be silly, Kaylee. Why would he be?

Gina took another deep breath, reached into the hole, and pulled out a small package wrapped in oilcloth. She held it reverently in both hands while her breath came in quick gasps.

"Are you okay?" Kaylee asked.

Gina tore her gaze from the package to Kaylee. "I'm not sure what to do with it."

Chad snorted. "That's easy. Open it."

Tears sprang to Gina's eyes, and she blinked quickly. In Kaylee's view, Chad had just gone from being a hero back to being a goat.

"Do you want some privacy, Gina?" Kaylee asked. "We can leave you alone for a few moments."

Gina seemed to consider Kaylee's offer, but shook her head. "I want you with me. Both of you. But . . ." She hesitated and her gaze swept the alley.

"Not here," Kaylee finished for her.

"No." Gina smiled, apparently relieved that Kaylee understood how she was feeling.

"The café?" Kaylee suggested. "Or we could go to my SUV."

Chad stepped forward and put his arm around his sister. "How about I treat us all to coffee? It's freezing out here."

"I'd like that." Gina smiled up at him then turned to Kaylee. "Let's go to the café."

"The café it is." Kaylee's gaze met Chad's and he gave her a sheepish smile. From goat back to hero in under five seconds.

Would the real Chad Sinclair please stand up?

The wrapped package lay in the middle of the square table, an object of curiosity for Kaylee and apparently an object of reverence for Gina. They sat in silence while the waitress poured steaming coffee into heavy white mugs.

Kaylee added sweetener to her cup and enough cream to lighten the brew from ebony to honey brown. Chad left his black and took a careful sip.

"That's strong," he said. "Just the way I like it."

Gina ignored hers. "I don't know why I'm so nervous."

"This is Jake's last gift to you," Chad said in a soothing voice. "And an unexpected one at that." He laughed softly. "You could be like Monk. You remember that detective show?"

"One of my favorites," Kaylee said. The lead actor had been brilliant as the San Francisco detective with obsessive-compulsive disorder.

"He waited years to open his wife's last gift to him," Chad reminded his sister.

A small smile lifted the gloom from Gina's expression. "I don't plan on doing that."

Chad pushed the package a few inches in her direction. She wiped the palms of her hands against her jeans, then removed the oilcloth to reveal a blue tin. The scene on the lid depicted a red-striped chaise with matching umbrella near a seashore. Colorful flowers adorned the foreground and the logo of Le Soleil, a premier Belgian chocolate company, resembled a bright summer sun.

The tin was familiar, but Kaylee couldn't place why.

"All this suspense for chocolates?" Chad shook his head.

"I never realized Jake had a flair for the dramatic."

He said it lightly, but Kaylee thought she detected a sense of relief in his voice. But that had to be her imagination, the lingering result of her early morning impression of Chad. And perhaps her tendency to see mysteries where none existed. Reese was right about that.

At least this candy tin had nothing to do with murder.

6

Kaylee stared at the contents of the tin, smiling as she identified the pressed flower—coarsely toothed leaves and white petals with their bright yellow centers—nestling in silver tissue paper.

"It's a *Fragaria ananassa,*" she exclaimed.

"Frag what?" Chad asked.

"I expected chocolates," Gina murmured.

"A strawberry plant," Kaylee turned to Gina. "Does it mean something?"

"Jake hated strawberries." The young widow sat back in her chair, clearly disappointed by the contents of the cache. "He never ate them. Why would he do this?"

Chad opened his mouth as if to say something, but took another sip of his coffee instead.

Kaylee racked her mind for something comforting to say. Unable to come up with anything that didn't sound trite, she fell back on her knowledge of botany.

"The accurate classification is *Fragaria* crossed with *ananassa.* It's a European hybrid dating back to the eighteenth century."

Realizing she'd slipped into her professor voice, she flushed.

"Interesting," Chad said, his tone making it clear what he really thought of the impromptu botany lesson.

Like a windup toy that couldn't stop until it ran down, Kaylee continued, "You write it '*Fragaria x ananassa.*'"

By that time, Chad had given up any pretense of listening to her. "I don't know about you ladies," he said, "but I've got other things to do today. Past time to get back to the shop."

"Are you going to look at my car?" Gina asked.

"First thing." He stood and pulled out his wallet. "I'll take care of the check on my way out."

"Thanks for the coffee," Kaylee said. A dull ache was taking root at the back of her head. She wanted to get back to Turtle Cove too, but Gina seemed incapable of movement. After getting Chad's assurance about her car, she had leaned forward, resting her forehead on the heels of her hands.

"Anytime," Chad said. He glanced at his sister, but apparently decided to leave her be. He half-shrugged in Kaylee's direction, the gesture clearly indicating he'd done all he could, then headed for the cash register.

Kaylee stared after him then focused on the café's wall clock. It wasn't even ten thirty yet. It was plenty early enough to get back to The Flower Patch, help Mary with orders, eat a quick lunch, then get a start on Jessica's displays. She could spare more time for Gina to work through whatever was going on inside her heart.

The clock slowly ticked off the seconds. Their waitress stopped by with a full coffeepot. "Ladies?"

Before Kaylee could answer, Gina piped up. "None for me. I'm ready to go."

"You sure?" Kaylee asked, surprised by the sudden shift in Gina's demeanor.

"No need to brood over something that can't be changed. I just don't understand why Jake chose a strawberry, that's all."

"It's a lovely plant," Kaylee said. "Delicate and fragile. Perhaps it reminded Jake of you."

"You think I'm delicate and fragile?" Gina didn't bother to disguise her scorn.

"I think you're hurting. And I'm sorry for that."

Gina removed the tissue paper from the tin, careful to protect the pressed flower. "You think that's how he saw me?"

She didn't seem to be expecting an answer, so Kaylee didn't

give one. She glanced from the flower to the tin, her attention caught by a blue piece of paper.

"I think he left you a note." Kaylee gestured toward the tin.

Gina snatched at the paper then quickly unfolded it. After scanning the page, she frowned.

"It's another clue."

They discussed the second note ad nauseam on the drive home. By the time Kaylee dropped Gina off at her home, Jake's words were trampling through her head like a song that wouldn't go away. The endless loop continued while she drove to The Flower Patch.

Roses are red, violets are blue

This strawberry is only for you.

At the chambered nautilus

You'll know what to do.

To find the next clue.

The rhythm was off, childishly so, but she supposed Jake had done his best. Though perhaps he should have been less cryptic since Gina didn't seem to have any idea where to go for the mysterious next clue.

The young widow had been despondent, maybe even a little angry, when she slid out of the SUV. Kaylee made a mental note to call her later just to be sure she was okay.

By now, the dull ache had spread to Kaylee's temples, and she was half tempted to pick up Bear from the shop and head home to Wildflower Cottage. But she couldn't leave Mary alone for the rest of the day, nor neglect her responsibilities. It was, perhaps, the only downside to owning her own business. Sick days were a luxury she couldn't afford, especially when she didn't really need one.

She drove past the front of the mansion and noted that Reese and his ladder were gone. No surprise, really. Like her, he had a long to-do list. She would have liked to talk to him about the note, though. He was a guy—maybe he could decipher Jake's clue. She scoffed at the thought. Reese was nothing like Jake.

Not that she had known Jake.

Oh, never mind!

After parking the SUV, Kaylee entered the mansion through the back entrance. Bear rushed to greet her, and she scooped him up in her arms. His puppy kisses were better than a painkiller any day.

By the time she entered the showroom, Bear's emphatic affection had her in fits of giggles.

"You're back," Mary said. "Just in time to meet Turtle Cove's newest resident."

"Only temporarily." The woman extended her hand to Kaylee. "I'm Whitney Mills."

"Kaylee Bleu."

"I know. Mary has been telling me about you. I met your grandmother a couple of times. Not that I was at all interested in gardening back then. Or flowers. But I've fixed both of those flaws." She smiled and gazed around the showroom, then yelped when she saw the clock. "Excuse me, ladies, but could I have a glass of water? I'm getting over a nasty sinus infection, and I'm late taking my medication for it." Mary ran to get her water, and

Whitney rooted around in her purse, eventually coming up with a prescription bottle. "Phew! I thought I'd lost it again there for a second."

When Whitney had swallowed her pill, Kaylee said, "You said you've met my grandmother. You've lived here before?"

"My parents spent the summer here once." For a brief moment, Whitney appeared lost in her own thoughts. "Seems like ages ago."

"Well, we're glad you're back," Mary said warmly. She turned to Kaylee. "Whitney is a public relations expert. The state hired her for a winter tourism campaign."

"For Turtle Cove?" Kaylee asked. She straightened Bear's red plaid bow tie and then set him on the floor.

"For the entire island," Whitney said. "Right now I'm scouting locations. Of course there are the typical places to highlight. But I'm also looking for the unusual, the 'you can't do this anywhere else' kinds of things."

"Sounds like a fun challenge," Kaylee said.

"This mansion for example. We could include it in a promotion for a tour of the historic downtown. In fact," Whitney continued, leaning forward, "it could be the showpiece. I can see it now. We start with a shot of the mansion, pull back to show the other shops on this street, all decorated for the holidays, then end with the mansion again. What do you think?"

Kaylee couldn't help smiling at Whitney's contagious enthusiasm. "I think it sounds great."

"Wonderful. That means I've found my first storyboard piece. And I haven't even been here twenty-four hours."

"It's the magic of the island," Mary said in her best otherworldly voice. "Creativity and imagination flourish here. The brisk sea breeze enlivens the blood."

"While freezing our fingers and toes," Kaylee added.

Whitney chuckled and glanced around the room again. "This could be good for your local vendors too, Kaylee. All the lavender-related products can be showcased. Orcas Island is more than whales and—" She paused in thought, then laughed, a musical, infectious laugh. "I'll figure it out. Are you free anytime tomorrow?"

Kaylee checked her calendar. "I have an appointment tomorrow afternoon, but the morning is flexible."

"Great! Shall we meet at that cute little bakery next door for coffee? I'll show you a few preliminary plans, and perhaps you could be my source for any floral arrangements or staging I might need."

Kaylee shared a glance with Mary. They were already swamped, but how could she turn down such a once-in-a-lifetime opportunity? "Sure, we can do that. What do you have in mind?"

"I'm not sure yet. Feel free to bring ideas with you. Around ten?"

"Sounds great." Kaylee penciled in the appointment.

"See you then," Whitney said. "Thanks again, Mary, for showing me around. And for recommending these soaps." She held up a small bag. "I can't wait to slip into a hot bath and surround myself with this luscious scent."

As soon as the door closed after Whitney, Mary beamed at Kaylee. "I love it when a big order just walks through the door. It's so exciting."

"And scary. I suppose she'll want poinsettias. Maybe mistletoe. That would be fun. What else?"

"Let's make a list of suggestions." Mary grabbed her notebook and pen. "Another profitable holiday season for The Flower Patch. Your grandmother will be so proud."

"It's not like I did anything. Did you know Whitney from when she was here before?"

"Just the Mills name," Mary said. "She comes from money.

Big money. If I remember right, the last time they were here was the summer that boy died."

"What boy?"

"The Glasser boy. Let me think a minute. What was his name? Dwayne, Darrell, no, that's not right." Mary snapped her fingers. "Derek. Derek Glasser."

Could Mary be talking about Gina's boyfriend? Reese hadn't mentioned his name.

"I heard Gina was dating someone else before she married Jake. Someone who died. Was that Derek?"

Mary's eyes widened. "I'd totally forgotten that connection, but yes. I believe they were dating."

The two women stared at each other, then Mary forced a self-conscious laugh. "It's a coincidence, that's all. A tragedy."

"I'm not sure I believe in coincidences," Kaylee said. "What exactly happened?"

"No one really knows. He was found in his skiff, which was floating out near the old pier."

"Where's that? I don't think I've heard of it."

"That's not a surprise. It's on the other side of West Sound in a secluded cove. We used to go there for picnics and swimming when I was a girl, but it's all overgrown now and hard to get to unless you know exactly where it is. And even though we still call it the 'old pier,' it's really nothing more than a few boards jutting out into the water. The pilings were in bad repair then. I can't imagine what they'd be like now."

"What was Derek doing out there?"

"No one knows. I don't think the police ever found anything. Not that I heard of anyway."

"How did he die?"

"It's been so long ago now. I think he hit his head. I guess he could have slipped getting into the skiff." Mary narrowed her eyes suspiciously. "Why are you asking me all these questions?"

"Just curious."

"Because he was Gina's boyfriend?"

"It's a little weird, that's all. First her boyfriend, now her husband."

"I suppose I shouldn't be surprised you're curious. You want a new mystery to solve, so you're grabbing on to this one. Except there isn't a mystery, Kaylee. Derek died, and it was very sad. Jake died, and that's sad too. But it's nothing more than a coincidence that they were both involved with Gina."

"I'm sure you're right," Kaylee admitted. Reese had said almost the exact same thing last night—that she was seeing mysteries where they didn't exist.

But could they blame her? She'd had enough mysteries to last a lifetime since moving to Turtle Cove.

"Speaking of Gina, did you find anything at the ferry landing?"

"We found a metal box hidden behind a brick in the back wall of a swimwear shop."

"How did you do that?"

Kaylee described their search and the crude symbols carved into the loose brick. Mary listened without interruption while Kaylee told her about the pressed strawberry flower hidden inside the tin.

"There was another note. A poem."

Just as Kaylee was about to recite the poem, Mary's phone rang. She gave an apologetic smile and answered the call. While she was on the phone, Kaylee scanned the order sheet. If she wanted to get home at a decent time this evening, she needed to get to work. Her conversation with Mary could easily continue while they put together a few of the arrangements.

Now they needed to come up with a few ideas for Whitney too.

While she waited for Mary to finish her call, Kaylee gathered the vases she needed for three of the orders. As she prepared the vases, she did her best to put Gina, and Jake's and Derek's tragic deaths, out of her mind. Instead she focused on her work and let her mind wander with ideas for potential Christmas arrangements.

Mary scurried into the workroom a few moments later, one arm already in her coat sleeve. "I'm so sorry, Kaylee, but I've got to run. That was my neighbor Joan. Her husband may have had a stroke. The EMTs have taken him, and she's all alone."

"Go," Kaylee urged. "And please let Joan know I'm thinking of her."

"I will." Mary finished buttoning her coat and retrieved her keys. "See you in the morning."

"Text me any updates, okay?"

Mary nodded and bolted out the door.

Talking to Mary about the poem could wait till tomorrow. Until then, Kaylee would have to do her best to figure out Jake's strange clue on her own.

7

The next morning, Kaylee studied Whitney's portfolio pad, intrigued by the rough sketches. The two women sat at a table inside Death by Chocolate. Kaylee had opted for tea while Whitney chose coffee. A small tray of assorted pastry bites took up the center of the square table.

"Like I said yesterday," Whitney said, "the mansion will be the establishing shot for this particular promo. Then the camera will take a stroll down Main Street toward Shoreline Drive to highlight a few of the other businesses. All the while, Christmas music will play in the background."

Kaylee was gratified to see that the storyboard sketches included both Jessica's bakery and Between the Lines, DeeDee's mystery bookstore. The ladies of the Petal Pushers garden club would be fully represented in Whitney's campaign.

"I met Jessica when I arrived," Whitney said, "and I've already talked to her about setting up a display on the sidewalk outside the store. You know, with mugs of coffee and cocoa, all kinds of baked goods. She loved the idea."

"It sounds wonderful. When do you plan to film?"

"We're on a tight schedule, tighter than I normally agree to. But the company the state originally contracted backed out at the last minute." Whitney leaned forward and lowered her voice to a conspiratorial whisper. "It's very hush-hush, but apparently their CEO was embezzling funds."

Kaylee's eyes widened, but before she could respond, Whitney rushed on.

"Anyway, I was a last-minute replacement. I hadn't even put

a bid in for the project, but sometimes these things come down to who you know can get the job done in a pinch. And that's me." She flipped through her notes. "The Thanksgiving holiday put a bit of a crimp in our schedule, so the camera crew will be here on Wednesday to do preliminary shooting."

Kaylee gasped. "You mean Wednesday like *tomorrow*?"

"I told you. The schedule is tight."

"I better get cracking on Jessica's window displays then."

"You've got a little time. We'll do this shoot on Saturday." Whitney tapped the storyboard. "What about these other businesses? Do you decorate them too?"

"I provide the flowers and plants for Between the Lines and The Chic Boutique. But that's it."

Whitney scribbled in her notebook. "Good to know. And if the other businesses need a little help? Would you be available?"

"If they want it, yes. But I doubt they will."

"You have a designer's eye, Kaylee. Not everyone does. Can I count on you to make sure this stroll down Main Street is a success?"

"You can count on me to . . ." Kaylee paused and bit the inside of her lip. "To soothe any ruffled feathers to the best of my ability."

"Anybody's feathers in particular?"

Sylvia Rosenthal and her sister.

Neither of the owners of The Chandlery Gift Shop would be thrilled to have their sense of good taste challenged by an outsider like Whitney. Or Kaylee either for that matter. But she couldn't say so out loud. Sometimes the best way to avoid trouble was to not suggest trouble.

"I think you'll be fine, Whitney. And these owners have been decorating their stores since long before I arrived. They're always beautiful."

"Loyalty." Whitney nodded her head. "I like it."

Before Kaylee could respond, someone called her name from near the bakery door. She glanced up to see Gina coming toward her with the blue tin in her hands.

"Mary told me I could find you here," Gina said as she approached the table. "I hope I'm not interrupting."

She glanced at Whitney then did a double take. Her expression froze, and Whitney's unflappable poise seemed to falter.

"What are you doing here?" Gina demanded.

A practiced smile spread across Whitney's face. "Why, I remember you. Aren't you Gina Sinclair? I think we might have gone boating together once or twice."

Gina's posture remained stiff and her knuckles were white as she clutched the tin. "It's Gina Beckett now," she said, her voice cracking. "Jake and I got married."

"Did you really?" Whitney's smile grew even wider though it lacked warmth. "How is Jake?"

Gina's face drained of color.

Kaylee quickly jumped up, grabbed an empty chair from a nearby table, and assisted Gina into it before facing Whitney.

"Jake recently died," she said in a low voice. "He had a heart attack."

Whitney's hand fluttered to her chest. "Jake's dead? Oh, Gina, I'm so sorry. I didn't know."

"I'm sure you are," Gina said, her voice flat.

Kaylee sipped her tea as the uneasy undercurrent between the two women became increasingly obvious. They had a past, and she couldn't help but think it had something to do with Derek Glasser.

A love triangle, perhaps? After all, Mary had said Whitney was on the island the same summer that Gina's boyfriend had died.

"I'm afraid I haven't kept up with island news," Whitney said.

"It seems a lifetime ago since I was last here."

"What are you doing here now?" Gina asked without a hint of welcome.

"Working," Whitney said. "I'm creating a winter tourism campaign for the state. Kaylee is helping me."

Gina turned her gaze to Kaylee with a hint of suspicion.

"I'm doing what I can," Kaylee said. She wasn't sure why she felt the need to explain, but something about Gina's expression made her feel defensive. "You know, with the flowers and the window displays."

When Gina didn't respond, Kaylee realized Whitney was staring at the tin. Gina seemed to notice too, and she clutched the tin even closer.

Kaylee sensed a subtle change in Whitney's demeanor. She moved with unnatural stiffness as she focused on adding a packet of sweetener to her half-empty coffee cup. But more than once her gaze drifted to the tin clutched in Gina's hand.

Kaylee stared past Whitney to where Jessica was clearing a nearby table. As soon as Jessica glanced her way, Kaylee sent her a silent plea for help. Jessica immediately came to the table with her usual cheery smile.

"Hi, Gina," she said. "May I get you something? How about my new holiday blend?"

"I'm not staying." Gina stood, and Jessica's gaze lowered to the tin box.

"Oh wow! The Le Soleil commemorative tin. I remember selling those a few years ago."

Gina looked doubtfully from Jessica to the tin and back again. "You did?"

Kaylee snuck a glance at Whitney who stared at her cup, her mouth set in a grim line.

"They were meant to be a keepsake," Jessica said. "Though I

don't think they're valuable. Did you get it here?"

For a moment, Kaylee didn't think Gina was going to answer. But as Kaylee opened her mouth to say something—though she wasn't sure what—Gina spoke up.

"Actually, I found it."

"It's in very good condition," Jessica said. "Someone took care of it."

"I suppose so," Gina said. She seemed to be having an inner debate with herself. Finally, she lifted her gaze to Jessica's. "Do you know . . . do you remember if Jake bought one?"

Jessica seemed momentarily taken aback by the question, but she quickly recovered. She took one of Gina's hands between her own. "I suppose he could have, but I don't really know. We sold dozens of these tins that summer. The chocolates were so yummy."

Whitney seemed increasingly engrossed in the conversation, and Kaylee had an uneasy feeling she was hiding something beneath her polite facade. Perhaps Mary would know what it could be, though she didn't seem to remember much about that summer. Only that a local boy had died alone out in his skiff.

Kaylee inwardly shook her head. What did it matter? Whatever history Whitney and Gina might have, it had nothing to do with her. She certainly had enough other things to do rather than indulging in years-old gossip.

"We still carry that brand," Jessica went on. "Would you like a sample?"

For the first time, Gina slightly smiled. Jessica had that effect on people. She had a knack for making them feel comfortable and at ease inside her cozy bakery.

"No thanks," Gina said. "I don't think the chocolates have anything to do with the clue."

"What clue?" Jessica asked.

Once again, a flurry of emotions flitted across Gina's face.

Kaylee longed to jump in, but she had no idea how much information Gina wanted to share. Something about the girl, though, brought out an almost maternal feeling in Kaylee. She wanted to protect Gina from harm even though she had no idea what, if anything, might be threatening her. It was the same kind of feeling she had sometimes felt toward a few of her students . . . the ones who'd seemed lost or out of their element, the ones who didn't have anyone else to confide in or to advise them. Sometimes it was hard to draw the line between professor and confidante.

Gina's longing to receive as much help as possible apparently won out over any hesitation she was feeling. Without saying a word, she took the lid off the tin and held it out to Jessica.

"Read the note," she said.

Jessica shot a glance at Kaylee, and she gave a small nod.

"Okay." Jessica pulled up another chair from a nearby table.

Other than scooting her chair to make room, Whitney remained quiet as if not wanting to draw attention to her presence. But Kaylee could feel some unidentifiable emotion emanating from her.

As soon as she was settled, Jessica removed the note from the tin and unfolded the page. She silently read the contents.

"What does it mean?" she asked when she'd finished.

"We don't know," Gina said.

"Where did you get it?" Jessica asked.

Gina gave Whitney a sharp glance, then turned to Jessica with a smile. "Jake had left a note telling me where he'd hidden it." As she spoke, a note of superiority crept into her tone. "He planned it for our anniversary next month."

"How romantic!" Jessica exclaimed. "Like a scavenger hunt. I've always wanted to do something like that."

Kaylee made a mental note to pass this information on to Jessica's husband, Luke.

"Kaylee helped me figure out the numbers." Gina favored Kaylee with what could only be described as a smile shared with a best friend. "If it hadn't been for her, I wouldn't have known what they meant."

"Numbers?" Whitney asked.

Once again Gina stared at her before answering.

Yep, definitely an undercurrent of something going on here.

"They were in the first note," Gina finally said. "The numbers for the geocache location. Tell them, Kaylee."

Kaylee gave a quick summary of how they'd found the location and the tin.

"But we don't know where the second note leads," she concluded. "Or whether the pressed strawberry flower means anything."

Jessica silently read the note again. "Well, a chambered nautilus is a kind of seashell. There are certainly lots of shells along the shore."

"Let me see." Whitney leaned closer to Jessica and appeared to skim the clue before anyone could stop her.

Gina glowered at her, then glanced at Kaylee and shrugged as if Whitney's behavior didn't matter.

Kaylee gave her an encouraging smile while making a promise to herself not to get any further involved with whatever history the two women shared. "Perhaps it refers to a specific store along the beach," Whitney suggested. "After all, the first clue led to a store. I seem to remember visiting a few shops when I was here before."

"You might look out by the marina," Jessica said.

"What do you think, Kaylee?" Gina asked.

"It's worth a try. I don't know anything else to suggest."

"Can you go with me?"

Kaylee glanced at the bakery clock. "I have an appointment this afternoon. And a full day tomorrow. Maybe the morning after that."

"I'm headed out that way," Whitney said. "We could go together, if you'd like."

"I think this is something Jake meant just for me." Gina's tone might have been sickeningly sweet, but her accompanying smile sent a chill up Kaylee's spine.

Jessica excused herself to wait on a customer, and Kaylee quickly took the opportunity to say goodbye and return to the safety of her shop. She wasn't sure about the wisdom of leaving Whitney and Gina alone together, but if the women had anything to say to each other, well, perhaps they needed the opportunity to say it. And no way was Kaylee going to participate in that conversation.

Though she had to admit she couldn't help being a little curious about the reason behind their obvious animosity.

A few hours later, Kaylee drove to the other side of the island for her appointment with Ellie Montgomery, the owner of Shortcake Bistro. Ellie also ran a catering operation and wanted to talk to Kaylee about floral arrangements for a few of her holiday parties.

Kaylee had only been at the restaurant, located southwest of Moran State Park, once before. She and Reese had stopped in for a late lunch after attending a nearby estate sale where Kaylee had bought an antique curio cabinet for The Flower Patch. At the time, Reese had mentioned something about a fire that had once damaged a wing of the building. Since then, it had been rebuilt and changed owners a couple of times.

Ellie owned it now, and her restaurant shared space with an artists' gallery overseen by a local art cooperative.

When Kaylee arrived, she parked beside a rental car that looked exactly like the car Whitney had been driving. Kaylee had seen it in front of The Flower Patch yesterday and near Jessica's bakery this morning.

How strange. Whitney had said she planned to go to the marina this afternoon. What was she doing all the way out here?

Again, none of Kaylee's business. She grabbed her tote from the back of the SUV and headed inside.

Large double doors opened to a foyer which led to a rustic dining area. With lots of interesting nooks and crannies for decorative touches, the space provided a fun venue for a holiday party.

"Hi, Kaylee." Ellie stepped through swinging doors that separated the dining room from the kitchen area. A tall woman with untamed red hair and a smattering of freckles, she wore a tidy apron over a sweater and khakis. "Come on back. You're just in time for a tasting. We're finalizing our holiday catering menu options."

"Sounds appetizing," Kaylee followed Ellie through the doors. Inside the kitchen, a long table held an assortment of dishes including fancy deviled eggs, mini crab cakes, and lobster rolls. At a nearby stove, Ellie's sister and co-owner, Trina Evans, ladled fragrant chili into small bowls.

Whitney Mills leaned against a counter, a plate in one hand and a fork in the other.

"Hi, Whitney," Kaylee said. "I didn't expect to see you again so soon."

"My plans changed," Whitney replied.

"Oh good, you two have already met." Ellie handed Kaylee a square plate. "Before you try the chili, help me decide between the eggs. These are topped with capers and parsley. Those are shrimp and jalapeño."

"Please don't ask me to choose," Kaylee said. "They both look delicious."

"That's what Trina and I think," Ellie said with a laugh.

"Knowing us, we'll put both on the menu and then regret it when we're up to our eyeballs in egg yolks and our secret filling."

Kaylee sampled both eggs but couldn't make up her mind which one she preferred. Though it was hard to choose when her mind was more occupied with Whitney's surprise appearance.

Why had she changed her mind about going to the marina and driven all the way to this side of the island instead? Kaylee was positive it wasn't just her imagination that Whitney had not been pleased to see her walk through those swinging doors.

As the women sampled the other dishes and the delicious chili, Kaylee joined in their conversations about upcoming holiday plans and Whitney's ideas for the winter tourism campaign. After the sampling, Ellie offered to give both Kaylee and Whitney a tour of the art gallery.

"We're on the National Register of Historic Places now," Ellie said. "This used to be a strawberry barreling plant way back when strawberries were one of the island's main industries."

"*Fragaria x ananassa*," Kaylee said quietly as she thought about the pressed white flowers Jake had put inside the tin.

"What's that?" Ellie asked.

"Nothing," Kaylee said. "Only the scientific name for strawberries."

"Count on you to know that." Ellie chuckled. "Our resident forensic botanist."

"Your what?" Whitney asked.

"Kaylee used to teach at the University of Washington in Seattle," Ellie explained, "and she worked with the police as a forensic botanist. I have to admit I had no idea what that was when I first heard about it. But even here on sleepy Orcas Island where nothing ever happens, our Kaylee has solved a few mysteries."

"How interesting," Whitney said as she eyed Kaylee with what seemed to be a new respect. Or was that a wary look?

Kaylee tried to dismiss her suspicions. But she couldn't. Whitney was here because of what she'd learned about Jake and his clues at the bakery earlier in the day. Kaylee was sure of it. Could the next clue be hidden somewhere here at the old strawberry barreling plant? But why would Whitney know that? Or care?

And what about the "chambered nautilus" line? Unable to help herself, Kaylee glanced around to see if she could find one of the shells anywhere in the gallery. Or even an image of one.

Much of the artwork, painted by local artists, was of beach scenes or nature landscapes. Several featured the Old Cape Lighthouse, where the Petal Pushers held their meetings.

And also where the holiday Festivity Committee was meeting that evening.

One crisis at a time, Kaylee.

Other paintings depicted Orcas Island landmarks such as Mount Constitution and Turtleback Preserve. The ferry landing, with its bustling shops and ferries, was another popular theme. But Kaylee would have to examine each painting more closely to find a shell.

But Jake couldn't have hidden a clue in a painting. Could he?

Not if he wanted to be sure it was still here when Gina came searching for it.

Kaylee sneaked a glance at Whitney, who was admiring a set of sculptures featuring marine mammals. An orca soared high above the base where a trio of turtles basked near a log. Ellie was answering Whitney's questions about the piece.

While they discussed the artist, Kaylee wandered around the gallery. This afternoon wasn't going at all as she had planned. She couldn't talk to Ellie about her order until Whitney left. And Whitney didn't seem to be in any hurry to go. In fact, it almost seemed like she was trying to wait Kaylee out.

The longer Whitney hung around—as if she had absolutely

nowhere else to be or anything else to do—the more suspicious Kaylee became. Whitney had told her that the filming schedule was tight. And yet here she was, browsing the art gallery as if she had all the time in the world. As if the history of the strawberry industry was the most interesting thing she'd ever heard.

Kaylee joined Ellie and Whitney as they returned to the dining room.

"There was a fire here a few years ago," Ellie was saying.

"A fire?" Whitney's face paled. She gazed around the interior and spoke more to herself than anyone else. "That's why it's so different."

"You've been here before?" Ellie asked.

Whitney appeared flustered but recovered quickly. "I think I came here with my parents once."

"The east deck and restrooms were destroyed," Ellie said. "And naturally the smoke damage was awful. Practically this entire half had to be rebuilt." She gestured with her arm to encompass this area of the building. "But all that was before our time."

"It certainly seems to have a rich history," Kaylee said.

"Before the bistro and gallery opened, it was a fine-dining restaurant. Real fancy place. The Ch—"

"Look at the time!" Whitney gushed. "How did it get to be so late? I'm going to miss my next appointment if I don't get going."

"Are you visiting another Orcas Island landmark?" Kaylee asked. Whitney's schedule wasn't really any of her business, but she asked anyway. Because deep down inside she absolutely knew that somehow this historic building had something to do with the strawberry plant Jake had left in the commemorative tin. And she was also certain that Whitney knew something about it.

"As many as I can," Whitney replied. The smile accompanying her words was bright but insincere.

"I've got a busy afternoon myself," Kaylee said, trying for a sympathetic tone. "The history, the artwork—it's all so fascinating. But I'd really like to talk about your parties, Ellie, and figure out what you need."

"Absolutely," Ellie said cheerfully. "I can get so carried away when I talk about this place, I totally forget the time."

"You obviously love it," Kaylee said. "Believe me, I understand. I feel the same way about The Flower Patch."

"Someday I'd love to explore that mansion." Ellie raised her eyes to the ceiling with a dreamy expression. "All those rooms."

"Since you ladies have business to take care of," Whitney interjected, "I'll be on my way. Thanks for allowing me the opportunity to sample a few of your dishes, Ellie. I know my film crew would love to eat here."

"Just let me know when," Ellie said. "We'll make something extra special."

After Whitney left, Kaylee and Ellie settled at one of the dining room tables next to a large picture window. A clear blue sky promised a cold, crisp evening with no precipitation. The evergreens were picture-perfect with a smattering of unmelted snow decorating their branches.

"I love that you have the art gallery here," Kaylee said after Trina delivered a pot of cinnamon tea to their table. "It's such a lovely backdrop for your holiday parties."

"The regulars seem to think so. We have the Artists Guild each year and the Chamber of Commerce." Ellie mentioned a couple of other groups, counting each one off on her fingers as she did so. "And finally our own staff party. We'll need centerpieces for each of the tables for two of the groups, but I won't have final counts for another week or so."

"Not a problem," Kaylee said. "Anything in particular?"

"What would you suggest?"

Kaylee took notes while the women discussed various options

for each group's budget. When they'd finished, Kaylee packed up her notebook and pulled on her coat. Ellie walked her to the café's entrance where they chatted a few more moments before Kaylee left. She stood on the porch for a moment, then made up her mind and went back inside.

"Did you forget something?" Ellie asked.

"Just wanted to ask you a quick question. What was the name of that restaurant you mentioned? The one that was here before you took over."

"You mean the fancy place? It was called the Chambered Nautilus."

8

When Kaylee returned to Turtle Cove, she kept an eye out for Whitney's car. She had tried convincing herself that she was making a mystery out of a molehill. But Whitney had purposely interrupted Ellie just when she was about to name the restaurant. Kaylee hadn't imagined that.

For a reason Kaylee couldn't fathom, Whitney didn't want Kaylee to know that Shortcake Bistro was associated with two clues in Jake's note: *strawberries* and *chambered nautilus.*

Kaylee recited the silly rhyme to herself again.

Roses are red, violets are blue;

This strawberry is only for you.

At the chambered nautilus

You'll know what to do.

To find the next clue.

The clue had to be at the bistro. But where?

And what did Whitney know that Kaylee didn't? What was she hiding from Gina?

Kaylee turned onto Pacific Street just in time to see Whitney emerge from one of the local shops accompanied by a younger man carrying a large bag over his shoulder. On an impulse, Kaylee parked her SUV and jogged to catch up to the duo.

"Whitney!" she called.

The younger woman turned and quickly masked her initial displeasure with a smile. "My, my, we just keep running into each other today, don't we?"

Kaylee glanced at the man and he extended his hand.

"Manuel Carmona," he said. "Camera operator."

"Where are my manners?" Whitney exclaimed. "I must have lost them on the drive back from the other side of the island."

"I'm Kaylee Bleu."

"Kaylee owns the gorgeous Victorian mansion I told you about," Whitney said to Manuel. "You need to get establishing shots sometime tomorrow. I'll leave it to you and Kaylee to work out the details."

She turned on her heel as if to leave, but Kaylee reached out and caught her arm. "Before you go, could I ask you something?"

Whitney turned back, this time doing little to hide her annoyance. "I think you just did."

Kaylee expected such silliness from her freshman students, but not from a professional woman.

"It's personal," she replied simply.

Whitney gazed at her as if trying to gauge how important anything could be that Kaylee would want to say to her. But whether from curiosity or to get Kaylee to leave her alone, she nodded.

"I'll wait by the car." Manuel pulled a business card from his pocket and gave it to Kaylee. "Around eleven tomorrow okay with you?"

"I guess," Kaylee said. Her mind was too preoccupied with what she was going to say to Whitney to give much thought to an appointment with the camera operator. "We'll be open all day."

"See you then." He strolled away. The whistled strains of "Jingle Bells" followed after him.

"What can I do for you, Kaylee?" Whitney asked as soon as Manuel was out of earshot.

Kaylee still hadn't decided what to say. But if years of teaching had taught her anything it was that the best approach was often the direct approach.

"Do you know where Jake hid the next clue?"

Except for a slight stiffening of her jaw, Whitney's face remained impassive as she stared at Kaylee for a long moment.

"How could I possibly know something like that?"

"I don't know." Kaylee spoke softly. "But somehow I think you do."

Another moment passed, then Whitney narrowed her eyes. "Funny. You didn't strike me as the type when we first met."

"What type?"

"Every small town has at least one. The middle-aged busybody with her nose stuck here, there, and everywhere." Whitney crossed her arms and gave Kaylee the once-over. "I bet you have at least five cats keeping you company when you get home."

"Only a dog," Kaylee said, doing her best not to let any defensiveness seep into her tone. She hadn't expected this conversation to go well, but she also felt an obligation to help Gina as much as possible. If Whitney was withholding information that could help Gina find whatever Jake had hidden, Kaylee wanted to know what it was.

"That's right. The little dachshund I saw at your shop." Whitney's smile was as fake as an aluminum Christmas tree. "He's adorable."

"I think so," Kaylee agreed. "Whitney, if you know something that would help Gina—well, you don't have to tell me. But I hope you'll tell her."

"There's nothing to tell, Kaylee." Whitney pulled out her phone and frowned at the screen. "This has been a delightful little chat, but I really must run."

Kaylee stood on the sidewalk while Whitney tapped her screen then placed the phone to her ear.

The woman's denials had convinced Kaylee of one thing.

Whitney Mills was a liar.

Later that evening, the Petal Pushers gathered at the keeper's quarters of the Old Cape Lighthouse for their weekly meeting. Since they were coming in as the members of the Festivity Committee were leaving, several conversations were going on in the foyer. As soon as Kaylee managed to extricate herself from Sylvia Rosenthal—who wanted Kaylee to take her side on the committee's most contentious issue to date—she secluded herself in a cozy side room.

At one time, it had been the lighthouse keeper's bedroom. The Petal Pushers usually met in the main room, but it had been taken over this month by the community choir. This room, one of Kaylee's favorites, was tastefully decorated with two leather love seats before a brick fireplace.

Kaylee found Reese kneeling on the hearth and pumping air into the base of the logs with a set of old-fashioned bellows. He turned as she flopped onto one of the love seats with a groan.

"That bad, huh?" he said, laughing.

"Why aren't you on that committee?" Kaylee asked.

"I am."

"Playing hooky?"

"Nope. I finagled things a few years ago so I'm a subcommittee chair. And its only member."

"What subcommittee?"

"The decorating-the-Sculpture-Park subcommittee."

"You do that all by yourself?"

"Me and a few other guys. Handpicked, unofficial members so they don't get roped into anything else." He leaned back on his haunches and studied the flaming logs. "Think I've got it. You ladies are all set for the rest of the evening."

"So what's your recommendation?" Kaylee asked. "Should a Douglas or a Fraser fir grace the park? Because we just spent more than half an hour discussing the merits of each without making a decision."

"Here's my recommendation to you," he teased. "Don't take sides. And first chance you get, name yourself the chair of a subcommittee of one."

"I think it's too late for that." Kaylee shifted into a more comfortable position. "I didn't even get a chance to bring up my suggestion."

Reese shifted so he faced Kaylee, his back to the crackling flames. "What suggestion?"

"When I was a kid, the Petal Pushers decorated a tree in front of the lighthouse." She gestured toward the main room. "Everyone brought cookies and cocoa, and the mayor turned on the lights. I want to bring back that tradition."

Reese looked thoughtful for a moment. "Yeah, we don't do that anymore."

"Why not?"

"Because the Festivity Committee comes up with other ways for the town to celebrate the holidays."

"I don't understand all the secrecy. What happened?"

Reese gave her a mysterious smile. "Think we'll have a white Christmas?"

Before Kaylee could answer, DeeDee waltzed in carrying a cardboard drink tray with four large coffees. Wearing a blue cable-knit sweater and leggings tucked into ankle boots, she could have stepped out of the pages of a holiday catalog. Her blonde hair was pulled back into a French braid intertwined with a blue ribbon.

"Hey, Reese," she said. "I didn't know you were joining us or I'd have brought a coffee for you too."

"It's too late in the day for me to be drinking coffee," he said.

"Too late for me too," DeeDee said. "But I'm indulging anyway. Kaylee, how about you?"

"I shouldn't."

"But you will."

"You know me too well."

"I'll be going before the other two Petals get here," Reese said. "I know how secretive you women are about your gardening projects. Though I get the idea more gets discussed than plants and flowers. If only these walls could talk."

"It's a good thing they can't," DeeDee said with a laugh as Jessica and Mary entered the room. "We'd all be in trouble."

Amidst the greetings, Jessica placed a tray of goodies from her bakery on the coffee table while Mary arranged Christmas-themed plates and napkins. They selected a few treats as a thank-you to Reese for getting the fire going. He popped a small brownie into his mouth but took the rest of his goodies with him. Once he was gone, Kaylee sat beside Jessica on one love seat while DeeDee and Mary sat across from them.

Another Petal Pushers meeting came to order.

Though little formal business was conducted in the winter months, Kaylee loved these gatherings. Her grandmother had been one of the founding members of the garden club, and when she moved to Arizona to live with her twin sister, Kaylee had taken her spot. The other three women had quickly become her closest friends in Turtle Cove.

The club took care of gardening projects—none of them secret, despite what Reese had said—throughout Turtle Cove. One of their most important responsibilities was the care of the lighthouse grounds. They spruced up the landscaping every spring and made sure everything was prepped for winter before the first snowfall of the season.

While the women selected their snacks, Kaylee updated them on the Festivity Committee meeting. As she shared what Reese had said about chairing his own subcommittee, she put a chocolate croissant on her plate and tried not to think about the calories.

"This is the hardest time of year," Mary moaned as she picked up a petit four covered in pink icing with a tiny white snowflake on top. "Who can resist treats like these?"

"As if you have anything to worry about," Jessica scoffed. "I hope I'm always as fit as you are."

"It's the tai chi classes," Mary said. "Perfect for both physical and mental health. I wish I could talk you gals into joining me. I enjoy them so much, and I'd love to share them with you."

"I don't know how you find the time," DeeDee said. "I'm already swamped with the girls' school and church activities." She sampled a raspberry macaron. "Yum. I want these at my holiday staff party."

"Remind me later," Jessica said. "My calendar is filling up too. Not that I'm complaining. I love this time of year. It seems the candies turn out especially yummy, and I get to make so many fun holiday recipes."

"Enjoy all the activities while you can," Mary said to DeeDee. "Those girls of yours will be grown up before you know it."

"Isn't that the truth?" Jessica exclaimed. "I talked to Mila earlier today about getting family photos done for our Christmas cards."

As the conversation continued, Kaylee leaned back in her corner of the love seat and stared at the flames dancing amidst the logs. Her mind wandered to past Christmases with her family when she and her brother were still children and all the times they'd gone sledding and ice skating and even hiking on bitterly cold days. The festive memories warmed her heart, and she felt a deep inner peace.

"What are you thinking about, Kaylee?" DeeDee asked. "You seem lost in another world."

Kaylee shook her head to clear it. "I seem to be especially nostalgic this year."

"Happy Christmases, I'm guessing," DeeDee said.

"Very."

Jessica lifted her coffee cup into the air. "To many more happy Christmases to come."

They tapped their cups together in an impromptu toast.

"How did your meeting go with Ellie?" Mary asked Kaylee.

"Great," she replied. "Whitney was there."

"Whitney Mills? Why?"

"Scouting another location. At least that's what she said."

Mary arched an eyebrow. "Do you think she had another reason?"

"Yeah," Kaylee slowly admitted. "I do."

She brought DeeDee and Mary up to speed on the conversation she'd had with Gina and Whitney in the bakery that morning and then told them about her visit to Shortcake Bistro.

"I saw Whitney on my way back to The Flower Patch," Kaylee said. "I still can't believe I did this, but I asked her if she knew anything about Jake's clues."

"How could she?" Jessica asked. "I didn't get the impression she and Gina were friends. In fact, quite the opposite. There definitely seemed to be tension between them."

"That's what I thought," Kaylee said. "But I was afraid I was letting my imagination run away with me."

"What did Whitney say to you?" Mary asked.

"That she didn't know anything."

"But you don't believe her?"

"The bistro and art gallery used to be a strawberry barreling plant. And—"

"The Chambered Nautilus!" Mary interrupted excitedly. "Herb and I used to go there for our anniversary dinners before it closed. I should have connected those dots before."

"But Whitney told Gina to try the marina." Jessica's tone was full of indignation. "She sent her out there on a wild-goose chase."

"That scoundrel," DeeDee said. "What an unkind thing to do."

"I think she did it on purpose," Kaylee said. "And I think the clue is somewhere in the old barreling plant."

"Then we need to be the ones to find it," DeeDee said.

"What if Whitney already did?" Jessica asked. "We have to figure out a way to get it from her. Would that be stealing? Should we call the sheriff?"

The other three women laughed. Jessica had an amazing ability to create conspiracies where none existed. DeeDee often encouraged her to use her vivid imagination to write a novel, but so far Jessica hadn't been interested. She was too busy baking to sit down long enough to write a paragraph let alone an entire book.

"Until we know otherwise," Mary said calmly, "I think we should assume Whitney didn't find the clue."

"I agree." Kaylee absentmindedly swirled the coffee in her cup. Jake's note wasn't very specific, not considering the size of the building where the bistro and art gallery were located. It also seemed strange that Gina, an island girl, hadn't made the connection with the historic barreling plant and the Chambered Nautilus restaurant. But then again, she was only a few years out of her teens, and most teenagers probably weren't interested in old buildings and defunct restaurants.

"Do we know for sure Gina didn't find the second clue?" DeeDee asked.

"She hasn't," Kaylee said. "I talked to her on my way to the Festivity Committee meeting."

"Did you tell her about Whitney?" Jessica asked.

Kaylee shook her head. "She sounded so discouraged. And besides, what could I say? It's not like I have any real proof that Whitney knows anything. I don't want to cause trouble."

"I think trouble already exists between those two," Jessica said. "They glared daggers at each other at the bakery this morning and didn't seem to care who noticed."

"You did the right thing in not telling Gina," Mary said firmly.

"But what do we do now?" Kaylee asked. "I want to help Gina if I can."

"We find the clue," DeeDee announced.

"How do we do that?" Jessica asked.

"First, we have to make sure Whitney doesn't go back to Shortcake's." As a retired police dispatcher, there wasn't much that fazed Mary. "She probably didn't feel free to look around with Kaylee there. She'll want to go back, and she has the perfect excuse with that job of hers. So we have to make sure Kaylee gets back there first."

"Me?"

"Who else?" Mary said. "You found the clue at the ferry landing so you're the logical choice to find the next."

"If you go in the morning, I can go with you," DeeDee offered. "I've never been on a treasure hunt."

"I'm not sure that's what this is," Kaylee said. "Shouldn't we check with Gina? She'll want to come too."

"I don't think so," Mary said. "You said she sounded upset when you talked to her, and I don't think we should get her hopes up. If you find the clue, then you can give it to Gina."

"Except that Gina might know where to look," Kaylee said. "Now that we've narrowed down a location, she may know what Jake had in mind."

"I've been thinking about that," Mary said. "Maybe Jake didn't create the trail for Gina."

The same thought had been swirling around Kaylee's head. But it hadn't seemed real until Mary spoke it.

"He might have created it for Whitney," Kaylee said quietly. "Do you suppose they were in love the summer she was here?"

"Perhaps they were," Mary said. "Though they did a good job of hiding it. I don't recall ever seeing them together."

"If that's true, then what do we do?" DeeDee asked. "Should we help Whitney instead? Or stay out of it?"

"When have the Petal Pushers ever stayed out of anything?" Mary asked with a grin. "But maybe it's time we did. What do you think, Kaylee?"

Kaylee turned her gaze to the fire as if an answer could be found in the dancing flames. With her changeable moods, Gina definitely wasn't the easiest person in the world to befriend. But wasn't that the kind of person who needed true friends the most? Kaylee was certain her grandmother would think so.

The phone conversation she'd had with Gina earlier replayed in her mind. The young widow had sounded so disappointed, so distraught. How hurt would she be if they were right and Jake's clues were meant for someone else?

But what if they were wrong?

How could they deprive Gina of Jake's final gift?

"We find the clue," she said finally. "And we try to do what's best for Gina."

Even if that meant trouble with Whitney.

9

For the rest of the meeting, the women brainstormed ideas for keeping Whitney away from Shortcake Bistro as well as where Jake might have hidden the clue. Their ideas ranged from the outlandish—Jessica thought a pretend kidnapping might be fun—to the mundane. DeeDee suggested getting Whitney hooked on a mystery from her bookstore.

"Her camera operator!" Kaylee exclaimed. She rummaged through her purse and found the card Manuel Carmona had given her that afternoon. Once she found it, she held it up with a flourish. "He's supposed to come to The Flower Patch tomorrow to take establishing shots. He might know Whitney's schedule."

"Call him," Jessica and DeeDee urged at the same time.

Kaylee took a couple of deep breaths, then tapped the number into her phone. When Manuel answered, she gave her name. "We met earlier today."

"I remember," he said. "Are we still on for tomorrow?"

"Absolutely," Kaylee said. "I just wanted to double-check the time."

"Eleven, if that still works for you."

"Great," Kaylee said enthusiastically. "Will Whitney be coming with you?"

"I doubt it," Manuel said. "She has an appointment with that gal from the whale place."

"Do you mean Roz?" Kaylee prompted. "Roz Corzo?"

"That's the one." He chuckled. "Whitney wasn't too happy about it, but I have a feeling Roz doesn't take no for an answer when she's made up her mind to something. And she was adamant that her place be included in the tourism promo."

"But it's too late in the season to see whales."

"Like I said, Ms. Corzo is determined. Whitney is going out on that boat whether she wants to or not."

"You're not going?" Kaylee asked.

"I mostly do the stills," Manuel said. "The film crew came in this evening, so they'll go on the cruise with Whitney."

"Good to know. Thanks, Manuel."

"Do you need to talk to Whitney? I've got her number."

"No, that's okay. I'm sure I'll see her around town."

"See you tomorrow then."

Kaylee ended the call and beamed. "Whitney will be with Roz. That gives us at least a couple of hours."

"I'll meet you at The Flower Patch at eight," DeeDee said.

"It's a date."

"Tell you what," Mary said. "I'll send Herb out to the marina in the morning. He hasn't gone on one of Roz's cruises in a long time."

"He won't mind?" Kaylee asked.

"He'll love the intrigue." Mary's husband was a retired postal carrier who now volunteered with the local Youth Association.

Jessica gleefully rubbed her hands together like a villain from an old silent movie. "A spy. I love it."

"So do I," DeeDee said. "And now that that's settled, I need to get home. My lavender soap won't package itself, and I want The Flower Patch to have an abundant supply for the holidays."

Mary tapped the coffee table with her palm. "I hereby declare this meeting of the Petal Pushers officially adjourned."

The next morning, Kaylee opened the door for DeeDee. She carried a large basket filled with lavender-scented goat milk soaps, lavender sachets, and a few candles. A new bow tie for Bear was attached to the basket handle.

"That's adorable," Kaylee said when DeeDee handed her the blue-and-silver striped tie.

"It's nothing really," DeeDee said. "Just a bit of leftover material from the sachets."

"I wish I could create your nothings." Kaylee removed the snowflake tie Bear had been wearing and replaced it with DeeDee's. "He's so dapper, isn't he?" Bear lifted his head as if to show off his new fashion statement.

"Like a gent ready for a night on the town." Mary took one of the candles from the basket and inhaled the fragrance. "These are my absolute favorite."

"It took me three tries to get the formula just right," DeeDee said. "Candles seemed like the logical next step, and making them isn't that hard. But I'm not experienced enough yet for the quality to be consistent."

"That's probably an occupational hazard," Mary said. "Not that I'd know. I'll stick to arranging flowers."

"Glad to hear it," Kaylee said. "I need you. Desperately."

Mary grinned. "Always good to be needed."

When Kaylee had first taken over ownership of The Flower Patch, she'd often wished her grandmother had stayed in Turtle Cove. They'd have had so much fun as business partners. But since she couldn't have Grandma nearby, she was over-the-moon thankful for Mary's practical experience and innate good sense. Mary had worked part-time at the shop before Kaylee bought it, so she was familiar with all the ins and outs of fulfilling customer orders. The transition had been relatively easy with Mary on hand to guide Kaylee through the gauntlet of small business ownership.

"Any updates from Herb?" DeeDee asked.

"He called a few minutes ago," Mary replied. "Our dear Whitney and her entourage apparently operate according to their own schedule. They're late and Roz is not happy about it."

"What if she doesn't show?" DeeDee turned from Mary to Kaylee. "Will we still go?"

"They'll show," Mary said confidently. "Herb is a good mediator. He called Whitney for Roz. Found out they were all having breakfast at the diner. But they're on their way to the marina now."

"That gives us a bit more time," Kaylee said. "Even so, we'd better get going. Especially since we don't have the slightest idea what we're looking for."

"I'm as ready as I'll ever be." DeeDee donned her mittens. "Who's driving?"

Kaylee pulled out her keys and soon they were on their way to Shortcake Bistro, former home of the historic strawberry barreling plant. When they arrived, the parking lot was deserted except for a couple of cars that Kaylee recognized from her visit the day before. Most likely Ellie's and Trina's.

"Maybe the simplest thing to do is ask if they know where Jake hid the clue," DeeDee suggested. "After all, they may have been here when he did it."

"Great idea," Kaylee said.

They entered the bistro and Ellie hurried from the kitchen to greet them.

"Kaylee, what a surprise. I didn't expect to see you again so soon."

"This is going to sound strange," Kaylee said. "A friend of ours received a note, like a clue, from her late husband. It mentions strawberries and a chambered nautilus. So we thought maybe the next clue could be hidden here and perhaps you could help us find it."

"Wow," Ellie said. "This is like a mystery from your bookstore, DeeDee."

"That's exactly how I feel," DeeDee said. "Do you have any idea where it could be hidden?"

"I wouldn't even know where to begin. May I ask who's the friend? And the husband?"

"Gina and Jake Beckett," Kaylee said.

"The boat builder who died recently?" Ellie shook her head. "Wasn't that so sad? To die so young. And his poor wife."

"You know them?" Kaylee asked.

"Not really. I don't think they ever came in here. But you know how it is. They're both islanders, and you see people around."

"I suppose we could be completely wrong about this," DeeDee said. "But we don't have any idea where else to check."

"No problem," Ellie said. "Why isn't Gina trying to find the clue herself?"

"She's still grieving and asked for my help," Kaylee explained. "The first clue led to another and now we're stumped."

"I suppose it wouldn't be much fun to follow a trail of clues when your husband has just died," Ellie said. "Poor girl."

"Would it be okay if we looked around?" Kaylee asked.

"Sure. I'll be in the kitchen if you need anything."

Kaylee and DeeDee spent the next hour exploring the bistro's dining area and gallery. Once again, Kaylee operated on the principle that Jake had to hide the clue in a place where Gina could find it without too much trouble, but where no one else would accidentally stumble across it. But they didn't have any luck.

They returned to the kitchen to thank Ellie. She and Trina were busy prepping for the lunch crowd.

"You didn't find anything?" Ellie said as soon as they entered.

Kaylee shook her head. "I can't imagine where it could be.

And Gina seemed so puzzled when she read the clue. She said Jake didn't like strawberries."

"Jake Beckett?" Trina said. "He loved strawberries."

Kaylee couldn't hide her surprise. "Gina said he never ate them."

"I was a couple of years ahead of him in school," Trina said. "We didn't hang out with the same crowd, but my mom made strawberry shortcake every year for the school fund-raiser. Jake always bought at least three servings and ate them all himself."

"That's so strange," DeeDee turned to Kaylee. "Maybe he developed an allergy or something."

Or something. It seemed the more she learned about Jake the more contradictions she found in the man. DeeDee could be right. It was certainly possible he'd developed an allergy, but that couldn't be the only possible explanation. *Why would someone who loved strawberries no longer eat them?*

Perhaps Whitney would know the answer. But it didn't matter if she did. Whitney wouldn't be confiding anything to Kaylee, especially after their conversation yesterday. Kaylee nearly expected to hear that The Flower Patch was no longer going to be the centerpiece of the town's tourism promotion.

"What did the whole clue say?" Ellie asked. "Do you have it with you?"

"I memorized it," Kaylee said. "It's not that long." She recited the rhyme and Trina asked to hear it again.

"It reminds me of that old garden sign." Trina faced her sister. "Remember, Ellie? It was for the restaurant, so it had a huge nautilus shell as part of the logo. But it also had a picture of a strawberry plant on it. You know, as a kind of homage to the barreling plant."

"I vaguely remember that," Ellie said. "But that seems an odd place for Jake to hide a clue."

"Where's the sign now?" Kaylee asked.

"Same place it's always been," Trina answered. "Out back by the garden. We had it repainted when Ellie and I bought this place, but then we went with a different sign instead."

"That space used to be a small strawberry patch," Ellie said, "until we changed the landscaping."

"But the sign is still there?" Kaylee felt her pulse quicken.

"Sure is." Trina grabbed a towel and dried her hands. "Come on, I'll show you."

"Wait for me." Ellie put a lid on a bowl of freshly made chicken salad and shoved it into a refrigerator.

After everyone donned coats and gloves, Trina led the way out the back of the bistro to a sign embedded in a stone base. It was about two feet by six feet, and the base probably stood three feet high. The Shortcake Bistro logo was painted on a pale green background.

"You can see why we didn't attempt to move it," Trina said.

DeeDee walked around the sign. "Where would Jake have hidden the clue?"

"Perhaps he buried it," Ellie said. "But the ground is pretty hard this time of year. I'm not sure he could have managed it without one of us noticing, though."

Kaylee bit her lip in frustration. For a few moments, she had hoped they were going to find Jake's hiding spot. Though writing a clue about a sign that was no longer displayed was troubling.

It seemed more likely that the clue wasn't meant for Gina but for someone else who knew about the sign. Someone who would have seen it before it was repainted.

"When was the sign repainted?" Kaylee asked.

"Three years ago. Like I said, it was right after we bought this place. We worked hard to get the building and grounds all spruced up."

"I remember when you were doing that," DeeDee said. "We were all so happy to see the place being given new life."

While the women reminisced about the renovations and opening of the bistro, Kaylee walked slowly around the sign. The back was undecorated but had been painted the same pale green as the front. She ran her hand along the top edge of the base. Maybe it had a hiding place like the brick wall behind the beachwear boutique at the ferry landing.

From what Mary had said, Whitney and her family spent a summer on the island four or five years ago. That was before Ellie and Trina opened their bistro.

Kaylee mentally recited the clue to herself, then repeated the last lines.

You'll know what to do

To find the next clue.

What did Jake mean by that?

Kaylee stood by the sign and gazed around. The melting snow had left slushy mud puddles scattered across the ground. An outbuilding stood nearby but if Jake had hidden the clue there, they'd probably never find it. Besides, it seemed unlikely he'd have expected either Gina or Whitney to rummage around in someone's storage shed.

"The tree!" Trina exclaimed. "Remember the tree, Ellie?"

Ellie frowned in confusion for a moment, but then her expression brightened. "Of course. Why didn't I think of that before?"

"What tree?" Kaylee asked.

"The one where the wild strawberries grow. That one." Trina grabbed Kaylee's arm and pulled her to a nearby oak. "I never gave it much thought, but there's a carving in the bark.

It's crude, but it could be—well, see for yourself."

When they reached the tree, Trina brushed loose debris from the bark and pointed. "There it is."

Kaylee examined the trunk then turned to DeeDee. "What do you think?"

"It's rough, but I think it could be . . ."

"A nautilus shell," Kaylee finished for her.

She circled the tree, identifying it as a *Quercus garryana,* or Garry oak, then gazed up into the branches. "Do you suppose the clue is up there somewhere?"

"Only one way to find out," DeeDee said. "I'll climb it."

"I'll do it," Kaylee said. "If you hurt yourself, Andy would never forgive me. *I'd* never forgive me."

"We can get a ladder," Trina offered.

"Not necessary."

Kaylee pulled herself onto the lower branches then settled in a nook beside the main trunk. The snow dampened her jeans, and she shifted uncomfortably. Not that it did any good. She'd be wet until she could change clothes.

But from this vantage point she could see a hollow inside the tree. The edges were rough, as if someone had carved out the space instead of it happening naturally. She reached inside, hoping there wouldn't be any spiders or bugs interested in her fingers, and touched something hard. Another package?

At first it didn't want to budge, but she managed to grasp the edges and pulled. When it came out of the hollow, she discovered it was identical in size and shape to the first package they'd found. And it was wrapped in the same type of oilcloth, though this one appeared weathered and dirty.

"I found it," she called down to the women on the ground.

"I don't believe it," DeeDee said. "Out of all the places around here. It's a good thing you remembered that tree, Trina."

"It's one of my favorites because of the wild strawberries that grow beneath it," Trina said. "Though I've never had the gumption to climb it."

"It wasn't that hard," Kaylee said. She didn't want to admit it to the others, but she was more concerned about getting down than she had been about climbing up. "DeeDee, can you catch this?"

"What if there's something breakable inside?" DeeDee asked.

Kaylee gently shook the package and listened for any indication its contents were fragile. "I don't think there is," she said. "Here."

She reached down as far as she could and dropped the package into DeeDee's waiting hands. Then she managed to return to the lowest branch and swung to the ground. Her boots slipped on a lingering patch of slush, and she landed on her behind.

"Kaylee," DeeDee exclaimed while trying to stifle a laugh. "Are you okay?"

"I bruised my dignity," Kaylee replied ruefully.

"As long as you didn't hurt anything else," Ellie said matter-of-factly. "Your dignity will survive, and we'll never tell."

"I'm just glad no one was filming that," Kaylee said.

"Oh I don't know," DeeDee said. "It might have been a fun promo spot for Whitney's campaign. Or part of a bloopers reel."

Trina and Ellie helped Kaylee to her feet and DeeDee handed her the package.

"I don't suppose we can open it?" Trina asked hopefully.

"We shouldn't," Ellie said. "Though I sure would like to see inside."

Kaylee wanted to open it too. She could almost convince herself she was doing Gina a favor by doing so. If the contents were clearly meant for Whitney—for anyone else—then Gina would never have to know the package had been found.

But Jake had been Gina's husband. Perhaps it was best she knew the truth—whatever that truth might be.

If only Kaylee could be sure Jake's secrets wouldn't push Gina over an unseen emotional cliff. Would it be best for Gina to let Jake's secrets stay buried with him?

10

Kaylee navigated the roads back to Turtle Cove while DeeDee cradled the unopened package on her lap. The women had agreed, despite their curiosity, that Gina needed to be the one to open it. Kaylee didn't know Ellie and Trina well enough to tell them about Gina's mercurial temperament. Even so, it wasn't her place or responsibility to withhold the package. She'd give it to Gina, be there with her when she opened it if Gina wanted her to be, and provide any support necessary.

That was the best she could do in these circumstances.

"It's the right decision," DeeDee said. "Though I agree with you. This package looks like it's been in that tree for a long time."

"That doesn't mean it's not for Gina, though."

"Maybe Jake created the trail when they were first dating. Or engaged. And then he forgot about it."

"After all the time and effort he clearly put into it? That doesn't seem likely."

"I know," DeeDee admitted. "I'm just trying to come up with an explanation—any explanation—that might be plausible. And men do forget things. I told Andy to bring spaghetti sauce and pasta from the store yesterday, but did he? No. And he was right there. How hard could that be to remember?"

Kaylee chuckled. "Must be convenient to have a husband who spends his days at the grocery store." Andy managed the local organic market.

"You would think so, wouldn't you?"

Kaylee shot a smile at her friend. She was spending way too much time brooding on Gina and Jake and Whitney, especially when she had more pleasant things to think about—like Jessica's window design, and the burning question of the species of Christmas tree for the Sculpture Park, and the centerpieces for Shortcake Bistro's holiday parties. She and Mary should go over ideas for those this afternoon.

But first she needed to deliver the package to Gina.

"I suppose I should call her," she said.

"Gina?" DeeDee asked. "Maybe she could meet us at the bakery. Do you think it'd be okay if I was there? Oh I guess not. But I'm so curious to see what's inside."

Kaylee grinned. DeeDee always seemed to have it together—whatever "it" was. But then she had these delightful moments of spilling her thoughts out loud in a rush. The other Petal Pushers loved teasing her about those moments, and DeeDee good-naturedly laughed along with them.

"Hand me my phone," Kaylee said, pulling over. "We might as well see what Gina has to say."

The conversation didn't last long. Gina asked Kaylee to come straight to Jake's office at the marina. Since Manuel wasn't expected at The Flower Patch for another hour, Kaylee agreed. Then DeeDee called Mary and Jessica to update them on their find. Mary reported that Herb hadn't called yet, so she assumed he was still on Roz's boat with Whitney and her crew.

Kaylee made a quick detour to Wildflower Cottage to change into a dry pair of pants. When she and DeeDee arrived at the marina, she pulled in next to Gina's car in a parking lot not far from Jake's office. Though *office* seemed an optimistic term for the ramshackle structure located about fifty yards from one of the piers at the far side of the marina. A dilapidated boat hung from chains in one of three slots at the waterfront. Kaylee guessed it was a project left undone by Jake's untimely death.

"This can't be easy for Gina," she said to DeeDee. "All the

unfinished business she has to take care of."

"I can't even imagine," DeeDee said. "I heard talk around town that Jake was building up a decent clientele here."

"I wonder what Gina will do with the place," Kaylee mused. Jessica had mentioned the life insurance policy. That had to be a help. Maybe there was enough money that she wouldn't have to rush into making any decisions.

"Sell it, probably. She doesn't strike me as the business-owner type. Though both my girls have had her as a substitute teacher. They like her. Especially Polly. She says that"—DeeDee imitated her daughter—"'Mrs. Beckett really, really listens.'"

"She doesn't exactly strike me as that type either."

"I know. But apparently she's very good with children, especially the younger ones."

Kaylee knocked on the door and a voice from inside called for them to come in. The interior was brightly lit and comfortably cluttered with tables and chairs, a counter, samples of wood, brass fittings, and other paraphernalia, and shelves holding manuals, maps, games, and a few books.

"Definitely a guy's place," DeeDee said.

"I think it'd be fun to hang out here," Kaylee said. "I can imagine Grandpa sitting at one of those tables, playing checkers and talking about the tides and the fishing."

"It has atmosphere, I grant you that. But I'd rather hang out in my bookstore or Jessica's bakery. Cozy, comfy places."

Gina emerged from an interior office and joined them. "I prefer cozy, comfy places too," she said. "But Jake loved it here. I never quite understood the appeal, but I suppose it has a charm of its own."

"What are you going to do with it?" Kaylee asked.

Gina shrugged. "Got any ideas?"

"I wish I did. It's like a treasure trove in here."

"Maybe. I've looked up a few of the items online, and they seem to be pretty valuable. I suppose I could try to sell them."

"That's a great idea." Kaylee put as much enthusiasm into her voice as she could. Gina seemed sadder in person than she had on the phone. Then she had sounded eager for them to come to the marina as quickly as possible. Had something happened in the meantime?

"Why don't we sit down over here?" Gina led them to a table near the front of the room. "It was my favorite place to be when I'd come here with Jake. He worked and I studied. And stared out the window at the harbor." Gina's expression became pensive as she gazed through the glass panes. "I've always loved watching the harbor."

Kaylee and DeeDee joined her, and DeeDee placed the package on the table.

Gina turned her attention from the window to the package. "It's like the other one."

"Yes," Kaylee said.

"I don't understand why Jake would hide anything out there."

"Have you ever been to the bistro?" DeeDee asked.

"Field trips when I was a kid. You know, the whole history of the strawberry industry thing. I don't think the schools do that anymore. And I was there once after the fire to see the damage. Just like everyone else on the island."

"But not with Jake?" Kaylee asked.

Instead of answering, Gina drew the package closer and unwrapped the oilcloth. Inside was another Le Soleil commemorative tin, identical to the previous one.

"Maybe we should let you open this in private," Kaylee offered.

"Please stay." A sad smile curved Gina's lips for the first time since they'd entered. "I may need you to help me solve the clue."

"Maybe it won't be a clue this time," DeeDee said. "Perhaps this is the end."

"I don't think so," Gina replied. "Though I'm not sure why."

She took a deep breath then removed the lid. A pressed gardenia rested on blue tissue paper. The white blossom was brown along the edges but retained a hint of fragrance.

"*Gardenia jasminoides,*" Kaylee said. "Perhaps the Kleim's Hardy variety. They're typical for cold-weather climates."

DeeDee and Gina stared at her.

"Sorry. I slipped into professor mode again."

"And we love you for it," DeeDee said, a twinkle in her eyes. "Andy gave me a gardenia corsage for our senior prom. They've been one of my favorites ever since."

"I love them too." Gina lifted the gardenia from the tin. "They're like the nobility of flowers. So white and beautiful."

"I had never thought of them like that. In the—" Kaylee stopped herself before sticking her foot right into her mouth.

"'In the' what?" Gina asked.

Kaylee quickly came up with something else to say. "In the Gilded Age, men often wore gardenias in their lapels. At least that's what Edith Wharton says in *The Age of Innocence.*"

"Wasn't that a movie?" Gina asked.

"Before that it was a book."

"Never read it. Would you hold this, please?" Gina handed the flower to Kaylee. Then she removed the tissue paper and held up the sheet of blue stationery that was underneath it. "I knew it. Another clue."

She unfolded the paper and cleared her throat. "It says, 'Petals here and petals there. A stolen kiss upon the stair. Daisies scattered everywhere.'"

"Any idea what it means?" DeeDee asked.

"None. Nor did I know Jake had such a thing for flowers—or

had a poetic bone in his body." Gina placed the note on the table and picked up the tissue paper. She mindlessly folded it in half then folded it again and again. "To go to all this trouble. Even to pressing flowers. Why would he do that?"

"I wish I could tell you," Kaylee said.

"I thought I knew him," Gina said. "But it's like he had this whole life separate from anything I knew."

"What do you mean?" Kaylee asked, gut tightening. The deeper they went, the more she was convinced this trail of clues had not been meant for Gina.

"Oh I don't know. Just little things, I guess." Gina walked behind the counter and pulled a wine bottle from beneath it. "Like this. Jake didn't drink wine. He didn't drink at all. But here's this nearly empty bottle."

"Maybe it wasn't his," Kaylee said.

"That's right," DeeDee added. "It could have been anyone's. A client maybe. Or a vendor of some type."

"I suppose," Gina said doubtfully. She glanced at the screen on her phone. "I know it's a little early, but how about lunch? I only had yogurt for breakfast."

Kaylee checked her watch. "Sorry. I've got an eleven o'clock appointment at The Flower Patch."

"What about after?"

Gina sounded so hopeful that Kaylee couldn't bring herself to say no. "It'll have to be a quick one." Kaylee gave DeeDee a look that dared her to refuse. "You'll come too, won't you?"

"Why don't we meet up at The Sunfish Café?" DeeDee suggested. "If we get there about quarter to twelve, we'll beat the lunch crowd."

"I don't know how long my appointment will be, so save me a seat if I'm late," Kaylee said.

"Will do," Gina said with more animation than she'd exhibited before. "It'll be fun. And maybe by then we'll have come up with some ideas for where this clue might lead."

"You want to keep searching?" Kaylee asked. "I thought you'd had enough."

"I thought so too. But you found this clue when it seemed impossible. With your help, I know we can find the rest of them. And then it will be over, and Christmas will be here and maybe it won't be so sad if I have this unexpected present from Jake."

"I hope that's true," Kaylee said. More than she could let Gina know, she hoped that was true.

The time with Manuel went by in a blur as Kaylee talked to him about the Victorian mansion. He took exterior photos from several different angles, then arranged to come back Thursday evening for photos of the lighted window displays.

When she returned to the mansion after lunch with DeeDee and Gina, she tripped over a loose board on the steps leading to her back porch. Another item for her growing to-do list. She made a mental note to mention the board to Reese the next time she saw him.

Once inside, she greeted Bear with a hug. She straightened the bow tie that DeeDee had made for him, then headed for the showroom. Mary was hanging a festive holiday wreath on a wall hook.

"What do you think?" Mary asked. "Too many candies or not enough?"

"Just the right amount," Kaylee answered. Like all of Mary's creations, this one was perfection. The red-and-white peppermints, interspersed with miniature silver ornaments, added a spark of gaiety to the rounded evergreen branch. Red ribbons trimmed with silver edging provided the finishing touch. "It's lovely."

"Hopefully our customers will agree with you."

"What's next on the agenda?"

"No new orders, so we can work on Jessica's window or the centerpieces for Shortcake's."

"Jessica's window. Manuel is coming back tomorrow night to take outside photos of the mansion when it's all lit up. I'd like to have the bakery window done before he gets here. Maybe he'll take photos of it too."

"Great idea. Does that mean you're staying late this evening?"

"Not sure I have much choice. All this running around for Gina has put me further behind."

"At least you found the clue."

Kaylee had told Mary that much when she'd been at the shop before lunch. They'd had a few minutes to chat before Manuel showed up. But she hadn't had the time to tell her about the clue itself or Gina's strange behavior. She did so now as they cleared a space on the worktable to use as a staging area.

Mary unpacked the nutcracker soldiers while Kaylee positioned a miniature Norfolk pine.

"The clues seem so cryptic, don't they?" Mary said. "It's almost as if Jake doesn't want them to be deciphered."

"I doubt they're cryptic to everyone."

"You think he left the clues for Whitney." Mary said it as a statement, not a question.

"The tin contained a pressed gardenia. Do you know what a gardenia means in the language of flowers?"

"'Secret love.'"

"I almost said that right in front of Gina. Fortunately, I caught myself in time."

"Do you think Jake was in love with Whitney?"

"Maybe." The knot slipped on the bow Kaylee was creating, and she tugged on it in frustration. "I don't know what to think."

"Lavender roses have a meaning too."

"I know. 'Love at first sight.' And the lavender plant means 'caution.'" With all the lavender fields on the island, Kaylee had learned that little bit of trivia soon after she moved here. "I didn't think about the flowers in the first clue meaning anything, but now? Maybe they do."

Mary picked up her phone and tapped something into it. "A strawberry flower means 'perfect goodness.'"

"I had to look that one up too." Kaylee finished the bow and cut off a length of ribbon to make another one. "Do you think it was love at first sight for Gina and Jake?"

"I doubt it. Gina's a few years younger than Jake, but they both grew up here on the island." Mary shook her head. "Perhaps it would have been better if Gina hadn't found that first clue."

"I've been thinking that myself. And I can't help feeling a little afraid."

"Of what?"

"That at the end of this trail, Gina is going to find a broken heart."

11

After closing The Flower Patch later that day, Kaylee and Mary carried the items for Jessica's window display next door to the bakery. Bear followed along behind them.

"Sorry I can't stay to help," Mary said to Jessica. "The choir is practicing for the Living Christmas Tree program. But we made a diagram showing where all the pieces need to be, and Kaylee has photos on her phone too."

"We'll do our best," Jessica said. "But it won't be the same without the Mary touch."

"I made her pinky-swear promise to stop by in the morning to make any last-minute tweaks," Kaylee said. "I just hope you love it when it's finished."

"I know I will," Jessica said. "Both you and Mary are so talented."

"It's your bakery goods that are the pièce de résistance," Kaylee said with a laugh.

They said goodbye to Mary, and Jessica flipped her door sign to *Closed*. "Do you want a snack before we get started?"

"Maybe later. I'm afraid if I stop moving, I won't get started again."

"DeeDee was in earlier. She told me about finding the clue. Poor Gina. She's having such a tough time."

"Definitely," Kaylee said. "I don't know if we should even try to decipher the latest clue. Maybe it would be better to let it go."

"Is that what Gina wants?"

"Sometimes. She can't seem to make up her mind. I think part of her is afraid of what she'll find, but she's even more afraid of not knowing where the clues lead."

"What are you going to do?"

"Be her friend. Or at least as much of a friend as I can be." Kaylee set the Norfolk pine on the window shelf and fiddled with a few of the decorations. Each one was made of wood, just like the nutcracker soldiers. "I think she's lonely."

"Why do you say that?"

"Because she was eager to have lunch with two women almost twice her age."

Jessica laughed. "Oh, come on. You're not that much older than Gina."

"Older enough," Kaylee said firmly. "And we're definitely in different life stages. I don't mean to be unkind, but I had freshman students who were more mature than Gina."

"Perhaps they also had a better family life."

"Maybe. I don't really know anything about Gina's family. Though Chad seems a little odd too." Kaylee told Jessica about how he tried to talk her out of taking Gina to the ferry landing then showed up to help.

"That does seem odd," Jessica agreed. "I really don't know much about their family situation either. But it says something about their dynamics that her parents didn't stick around after the funeral."

"Do you remember anything about her boyfriend?" Kaylee asked. "The one who died a few years ago?"

"Not really. My daughter, Mila, must have been a year or two ahead of Gina in school. After she graduated high school, I wasn't involved in school activities anymore so I didn't know the younger students that well."

"That's understandable."

"I remember when the boy died, though. It shocked the entire community to lose one of our own like that. Such a senseless thing."

"Do you know what happened?"

"Only that he was found in his skiff. Just drifting along."

"What about the autopsy?"

"If I remember right, he'd hit his head somehow. There wasn't any reason to suspect foul play, so I don't know if there was an autopsy or not."

Kaylee started to protest then thought better of it. In the big city, an autopsy probably would have been a matter of routine. After all, the deceased was young, only a few years out of high school. His sudden death when he should have been in peak health would have triggered a full investigation. But she'd lived in Turtle Cove long enough to know that just because something was a matter of routine in a big city didn't mean it was in this small village where most of the people knew each other and wouldn't have assumed foul play simply because of the environment. Nothing bad ever happened in Turtle Cove.

Though that wasn't quite true. She'd certainly had her share of adventures since she'd moved here. Whoever said life in a small town was boring must never have set foot in this one.

Their talk turned to other topics as they finished decorating the window. Before long all the nutcracker soldiers, gaily wrapped boxes, and the festive dishes for the featured bakery items were in their proper places. For the final touch, Kaylee placed miniature train tracks around the Norfolk pine's base and added the engine and cars. When everything was just right, Jessica flipped the switch on the surge protector. The lights came on and the train moved around the track.

They went outside and stood in the center of the street, which was devoid of traffic, to see the window. Kaylee suddenly had a strange sense of déjà vu. Only a few evenings before, she and Mary had stood just a few feet away gazing at the mansion windows. That's when her adventure—if she could call it that—with Gina had begun.

"It's perfect," Jessica said, arms crossed against the cold evening air. "You've done such a great job."

"Mary did so much for it," Kaylee said. "She helped me stage everything so we could work out the kinks ahead of time. She's a great 'tweaker.'"

"Mary's a talented designer, but you don't give yourself enough credit. You're a talented designer too. And I'm thrilled with my Christmas window. It's never looked so charming."

"I'm glad you're happy with it." Kaylee beamed with pride. The setup made it easy for Jessica to switch out the bakery treats with ease so she could showcase a variety of holiday options. And Jessica was right. The scene was simply charming.

They were heading back into the bakery when a car rumbled up the street. Kaylee recognized it immediately as Whitney's rental car. Her shoulders stiffened, but she put on a friendly smile and waved. The smile froze in place as the car pulled to the curb and Whitney emerged.

"We need to work on our timing," Jessica muttered low enough for only Kaylee to hear.

"Agreed."

If they'd only gone inside the bakery a couple of minutes sooner, maybe Whitney would have driven on past.

"Good evening, ladies," Whitney said as she joined them. "Admiring your window?"

"We just finished," Jessica said. "What do you think?"

Kaylee braced for the inevitable criticism. After their conversation yesterday, she and Whitney definitely weren't the best of friends. The woman was sure to find fault with something.

Whitney stepped closer and scrutinized the display for several long moments while Kaylee and Jessica exchanged glances behind her back.

"Lovely." Whitney faced Kaylee. "You do exceptional work."

Surprised by the compliment, Kaylee's nerves eased. "Thank you."

"I'm glad I saw you here. This strange little idea has been roaming around in my mind, and I thought you might be able to help me with it."

"Sure. If I can." Kaylee couldn't help but be curious about the unexpected turn.

"Why don't we go inside?" Jessica suggested. "It's too cold to talk about strange little ideas out here. I can put the kettle on for tea."

"Thanks, but I can't stay long," Whitney said, "and this will only take a minute."

"What's your idea?" Kaylee asked.

"I was thinking about this geocaching thing you and your friend—Gina, was it?—were talking about."

Kaylee nodded, thinking Whitney wasn't as clever as she liked to imagine. Kaylee knew full well Whitney was aware of Gina's name. So why was she pretending she wasn't?

"It just seems like that would be a fun tourism promotion too." Whitney laughed a little too loud. "Not in winter obviously. I can't imagine how miserable it must be for the two of you to be traipsing around in this kind of weather looking for clues and hidden boxes. But it might be a fun spring or fall promotion. We could make it into an island-wide scavenger hunt, and each group could take what's in each location and leave something new for the next group."

"That does sound like fun," Kaylee agreed. She immediately considered, discarded, and flipped through various ways to organize such a huge event. But beneath the rush of possibilities, she sensed something behind Whitney's scheme. "How could I help?"

"I wondered if you could tell me again about the clues Gina

already found. Maybe we could use the same hiding places."

"I would rather not," Kaylee said. "Those are personal to Gina and Jake."

Even as she said the names, Kaylee faltered. If her suspicions were correct, the clues were probably more personal to Whitney than to Gina.

"I'm not asking you to break any confidences," Whitney said, her voice as smooth as the icing on one of Jessica's pastries. "There must be a knack to writing a good clue though."

"If the GPS coordinates are part of the clue," Kaylee said, trying to turn the conversation a bit, "most people should be able to find them without too much trouble. The first thing you need to decide is if you want to do a geocache trail or a scavenger hunt."

"What's the difference?"

"A scavenger hunt wouldn't include the coordinates."

"And the clues would have to be easy ones," Jessica added. "Especially if they're meant for tourists. Visitors won't know all the local lore and place names. Though it might be hard to keep islanders from participating, especially if you're giving away great prizes."

Whitney gazed up the street, and Kaylee sensed she was annoyed that the conversation wasn't going the way she wanted.

"You've both given me things to think about," she said. "I'd still like to see examples of clues, though."

"You'd have to ask Gina," Kaylee said. "They belong to her."

Whitney held Kaylee's gaze, and her eyes hardened. "You found the last one, didn't you? The one about the chambered nautilus."

Kaylee didn't avoid Whitney's stare, but she didn't respond either. She had nothing to say.

"What was it?" Whitney's voice faltered. "Another clue?"

"Why are you so interested?" Kaylee asked, keeping her voice as even as possible.

"Are you and Gina good friends?"

Taken aback by the question, Kaylee stammered her answer. "Not really."

"That's too bad." Whitney's voice, stronger now, seemed edged with steel. "A friend would consider that following these clues might not be in Gina's best interest."

"Would they be in yours?"

Whitney's gaze slid from Kaylee to the decorated window. "Stick to what you know best, Kaylee. I'll be in touch about the filming schedule."

Before Kaylee or Jessica could say another word, Whitney returned to her car and drove away.

"What was that all about?" Jessica asked.

"I wish I knew," Kaylee said. The problem was that she was pretty sure she did know. Whitney had practically confirmed Kaylee's worst fears.

To avoid any more heartbreak, Gina needed to stop following the clues.

But could Kaylee convince her of that without telling her why?

12

The next afternoon, Kaylee glanced at the wall clock and concentrated on not tapping her pen on the table while she waited for Aida Friedman, the main receptionist at the sheriff's department, to complete her call. Aida paced just outside the interrogation room while Kaylee, seated at the table, found herself frequently staring at the huge mirror hanging on one wall.

Even though she was sure everyone in the department had better things to do than watch her and Aida talk about flowers, the one-way mirror unnerved her. What if Sheriff Eddie Maddox was on the other side of that wall? They had a great professional relationship, and the sheriff appreciated having a trained forensic botanist on the island. Kaylee's knowledge and previous experience with Seattle law enforcement had served her well here in Turtle Cove on several occasions. The sheriff might find it amusing to watch Kaylee try to get a word in edgewise with the highly caffeinated, though amazingly efficient, Aida.

Or what if Deputy Nick Durham was behind the glass? He'd find it hilarious to spy on Kaylee without her knowing it. He would definitely be amused by her conversation with Aida. *What a nightmare.*

But it couldn't be helped. They needed a table so Aida could flip through Kaylee's notebooks of colorful floral arrangements. The receptionist's desk—already crowded with a computer, printer, and phone system—didn't have enough space.

Kaylee tapped the pen, stopped herself, then tapped it again.

Aida finished her call, entered the room, and popped a wintergreen Tic Tac—her pack-a-day vice—into her mouth.

"Great news," she said as she took a seat. "The coach's sister broke her leg."

"That's good news?"

"Not that she broke her leg. That's horrible news. I don't know how we'll beat the Portland Blades without her speed. Are you sure you don't want something to drink besides water? I'm getting another soda."

"I'm fine, thank you." The words were barely out of Kaylee's mouth before Aida disappeared again.

Kaylee tapped her pen and gazed at the mirror. Maybe she was the victim of one of those hidden camera television shows. Amused by the thought—how fun would that be?—she decided to play along.

Just in case.

She crossed her eyes, then stuck her thumbs in her ears and waggled her fingers.

"Having fun?"

Kaylee's attention snapped to the door. Sheriff Maddox leaned against the frame cradling a huge mug. *World's Greatest Grandpa* was emblazoned in large, thick letters across the front.

"How's the newest member of the Maddox family?"

"She's the most beautiful baby ever born." He pulled out one of the chairs, turned it around, and straddled it. "Not that I'm biased."

"Of course not."

He set the mug on the table and pulled out his phone. "I just got the latest photo."

"I'd love to see it."

Eddie and Susan's first grandchild had made her appearance into the world only a couple of months ago. The baby's parents lived in Idaho, so Eddie had stayed only a few days to celebrate the special event while Susan extended her visit a while longer.

During his wife's absence, the Petal Pushers had made it their mission to ensure the sheriff didn't miss any meals.

Kaylee oohed and aahed over the photos while Eddie beamed. "So much hair!" she said.

"And black as the darkest night."

"Just like yours."

"And my mother's." He beamed. "There's something—I don't even know how to explain it. But to see our Alaskan Native heritage in a new generation does something right here." He tapped his chest over his heart.

"It must," Kaylee said with a smile. "I've never seen you so sentimental."

"Don't tell anyone." The corners of his mouth turned up in a delighted grin. "It'll ruin my reputation."

"My lips are sealed."

"So what are you doing here? Rack up too many traffic tickets? Forget to buy a doggy license for Bear?"

"Nothing like that." Kaylee gestured at the notebooks. "Aida asked me to come so she could pick out flowers for the station's Christmas party."

"You got time to stop by my office when you're done here?"

"Sure. What's up?"

"I'm not sure, but I'm hoping you'll be able to help." He stood and slid the chair back under the table. "See you in a few."

Aida popped back in the door as the sheriff was leaving. She dodged around him in an elaborate maneuver that sent her shoulder-length blonde hair flying behind her.

"Good moves, Miss Demeanor," Eddie said with a laugh before disappearing down the hall. It was the perfect name for Aida's roller derby persona.

"Thanks, Sheriff," she called after him. "I expect to see you at the tournament."

"What tournament?" Kaylee asked.

"The one I was telling you about earlier."

"I don't think you did."

"Did I tell you about the coach's sister's broken leg?"

"You said you had good news, and that wasn't it."

"That's right." Aida slowly opened the cap on her soda bottle, releasing the fizz a little at a time. "She was in charge of getting the flowers for the tournament winners. But after she broke her leg she asked me if I could take care of them instead, and I said yes because I was already meeting with you. Two birds, one stone and all that."

"What kind of flowers do you need?"

"Long-stemmed roses. Three for each member of the winning team. They don't all have to be the same color, but each bouquet has to be identical. You wouldn't believe how competitive these women can be."

Kaylee couldn't even imagine.

"Do you have a preference?"

"Peach is always good. That's not a color any of the teams use for their uniforms. We don't want to look like we're favoring one team over another. As much as I'd like to go with our colors."

"Which are?"

"Purple and gold."

"Nice combination." Kaylee opened a new file on her tablet. "How about two peach roses and one white in each trio?"

"I like that." Aida popped another Tic Tac.

Kaylee finalized the details for the roller derby tournament order, then managed to keep Aida in the interrogation room long enough to get the order for the sheriff's holiday party too. She was tempted to handcuff the jumpy receptionist to the table more than once.

When they'd finally finished, Kaylee packed up her books and

Aida returned to her desk, where she hopped on her computer, fingers flying, then reached over to answer the phone on the second ring.

What Kaylee wouldn't give to have that much energy. But no way did she want Aida's nervous habits. Nor did she want to take Miss Demeanor's place at the roller derby. Maybe she should take Mary up on her standing offer to go to a tai chi class.

The door to the sheriff's office was open, but Kaylee rapped on the frame before entering. He rose and greeted her. "Come on in, Kaylee. Close the door, will you?"

"Must be serious. What's going on?" She settled in a chair opposite Eddie's desk while he resumed his seat.

"Wish I knew. Do you know Gina Beckett?"

"Not really. Though I've been spending time with her lately."

"Why's that, if you don't mind me asking?"

"Why *are* you asking?"

"I asked first."

"She found a letter, a clue, in Jake's desk at the marina. And that led to another clue. The first one included GPS coordinates, but she didn't know what they were. So she asked my help figuring them out."

"Why did she come to you?"

"She said it was because I have a reputation for solving mysteries."

"And you seem to be pretty good at it." A smile played on the sheriff's face. "Tell me more about this letter. Who was it from?"

"Jake wrote it. Gina thinks it might have been an anniversary present."

"Do I detect a hint of skepticism in your voice?"

Kaylee wavered. She didn't want to engage in gossip with the sheriff. But neither did she want to withhold information he might need to know.

Unable to make up her mind, she asked instead, "Is Gina in trouble?"

"I honestly don't know." He opened a folder on his desk and slid a sheaf of papers toward Kaylee.

"What's this?"

"Medical examiner's report. For Jake Beckett."

Kaylee stared at him a moment then scanned the document. "Giles didn't do the autopsy?"

Giles Akins, Orcas Island's elected coroner, was also the local funeral home director. He and his son usually handled any of the final arrangements needed by the islanders. But this document had been signed by a Seattle medical examiner.

"Giles was at a convention in Portland. The initial finding, as you know, was that Jake's heart gave out on him. Hard to believe for someone his age, but it wasn't a secret he had a weak heart. Kept him from playing high school football." Sheriff Maddox set his mouth in a grim line as he stared out his office window. Kaylee sensed his focus wasn't on the wintry landscape.

A moment later, he dropped a document in front of her. "Then I got the toxicology report."

Kaylee flipped to the correct page and skimmed the results. "Antibiotic overdose?" She stared at the sheriff. "Do you think Jake committed suicide?"

"The morning he died, Jake put a hefty deposit on an ice-fishing trip with a couple guys from the marina. The guys were talking about it at Jake's funeral. I doubt he'd do that if he had no actual plans to be there. And using antibiotics would be an extremely unusual way to kill yourself. In fact, I've never seen or heard about it."

"But if not suicide . . ." Kaylee winced, not wanting to even think the awful alternative.

"Murder, Kaylee. Jake Beckett was murdered."

Since Sheriff Maddox needed to tend to business while they waited for Gina and Nick to arrive, Kaylee retreated to the break room. Too fidgety to sit, she paced the room's perimeter, detouring around the empty tables. After her third lap, she succumbed to the lure of a soda and candy from the vending machines.

Even though it was right there in black and white, she was having a tough time believing what she'd learned from reading the Seattle medical examiner's report. Yet it had to be true.

After the sheriff's unpleasant revelation, Kaylee had told him about the letter and the clues, about Gina's fluid personality, and how the caches had been found.

But she hadn't had the chance to tell him about Whitney. While she was still debating whether or not to share her suspicions, the sheriff had received a phone call from Deputy Nick Durham. The deputy was bringing Gina in for questioning. Sheriff Maddox asked Kaylee to stay, thinking Gina might be more comfortable if someone she knew and trusted was with her.

Kaylee privately wondered if Gina might be better off with a lawyer, but the sheriff, like most law enforcement officials, wouldn't want Kaylee to remind him of that. From his perspective, if Gina wanted a lawyer, she could ask for a lawyer. The purpose of this meeting was to provide an update to a grieving widow on the circumstances of her husband's death. If Gina volunteered incriminating information, then perhaps they could get this case wrapped up before the weekend.

She might not agree, but Kaylee had worked with law enforcement long enough to understand his position.

She took another sip of soda as she made another lap around

the room, thinking that at least her nervous energy could help burn off some of the calories she was consuming.

Jake Beckett. Boat builder. Dead of an apparent heart attack though he was only in his twenties.

Except it wasn't a heart attack but a massive overdose of antibiotics, specifically azithromycin.

Someone had killed him.

But who?

Kaylee refused to believe Gina was guilty of such a horrendous crime. The girl was a little odd, true. But she had seemed utterly heartbroken after Jake's death. And she was still grieving.

In the months since Kaylee had moved to Turtle Cove, The Flower Patch had provided flowers for dozens of funerals. The range of grief of those left behind ran the gamut from deep sorrow to hidden relief to, on the rare occasion, indifference. A few mourners even attempted to display more grief than they felt.

But visitations and funerals were too emotional, feelings too raw. Those who tried to pretend couldn't keep up the pretense. They slipped, and Kaylee had learned to spot the fakers with ease.

Never would she put Gina in that small group.

The door creaked open and Deputy Nick Durham walked in. "Sheriff said I could find you in here. He's waiting in his office."

"How's Gina?"

"She's not saying much. I left her with Aida."

"Does she know about Jake?"

"Not from me." Nick held open the door for Kaylee and they walked along the hallway. "But she knows something is wrong. It's not every day a handsome deputy like myself comes calling. And when I'm in uniform, it's not because I'm there on a date."

"How did you get her to come with you?"

"Just said the sheriff wanted to talk to her. She didn't fight it." He tugged at his goatee, an unconscious habit. "Wish everybody was that easy to deal with."

"I feel sorry for her. She's so young to have to deal with something like this."

His expression turned serious as they neared the office. "It never gets easier, does it?"

Since Kaylee had moved here, she'd seen more death than she could ever have anticipated. "No, it never does."

Jake Beckett had died of an overdose of medication. In Kaylee's experience assisting law enforcement, that usually meant either an accidental ingestion or suicide.

There was another possibility, though, and Gina came immediately to mind. After all, didn't the police always investigate the murder victim's spouse first? And there was that insurance policy.

Kaylee hoped Gina was innocent.

But what if she wasn't?

13

Kaylee gave Gina an encouraging smile as they settled in their seats. Gina responded with a brief smile of her own, then shifted her gaze to the desk, the walls, out the window, as if she didn't know where to look or what she wanted to see. Or not see.

Nick leaned against the wall near the door, arms folded across his chest, as Sheriff Maddox retreated behind his desk and cleared his throat.

"I want to thank you for coming in, Mrs. Beckett," he said in his most soothing tone. "I hope it wasn't too much of an inconvenience."

"No, no." Gina's gaze flitted to him then darted away again. She played with the hem of her knit tunic and adjusted it over her black leggings. "I'm not substituting today. I'm not doing much of anything it seems. Unless I'm at the marina, at Jake's place."

Her gaze landed on her fingers, now intertwined in her lap. Her mouth curved upward for a moment, then straightened. "Jake's place. Never *our* place. It was always like that. Even when I was there it seemed I didn't quite belong."

She raised her head and stared at the sheriff. His expression stayed soft and unthreatening.

"Does that seem right to you, Sheriff? Should it have been that way?"

He tilted his head and one corner of his mouth lifted. "A lot of men—particularly a man like Jake who worked with his hands, who took pride in his craft—men like that see their workplace as a kind of retreat from the rest of the world. I don't think he would have meant it as a place where you would feel unwelcome."

"I suppose," Gina said, a wistful tone in her voice.

"He made it a friendly place though," Sheriff Maddox continued. "I've been in there a few times, talking to the old-timers who still hung around after Jake bought it. He didn't mind them coming in, playing their games of checkers. Telling the same fish stories over and over again."

His chair squeaked as he leaned back. "I know they were relieved it was Jake who took over the business instead of some stranger. One of our own who cared about the Sound. About doing right by others."

"That's what they thought of Jake?"

"I'd say so. At least that's the impression I always got whenever I was out that way."

"I don't know what to do." The pitch in Gina's voice rose. "About the business or anything else."

Kaylee rested her hand on Gina's arm. "Those aren't decisions you have to make right now. Give yourself time. When you're ready, you can sort through it all."

"Kaylee is right," Sheriff Maddox said. "Unless you need to make a quick sale for the money, just wait awhile. In a few months, all these decisions might not seem so heavy."

"That sounds like good advice. Thank you." Gina shifted in her seat toward Kaylee. "Would you mind if I rode back to Turtle Cove with you? He brought me, which is just as well because my car wouldn't start." She gestured toward Nick. "I've never ridden in a sheriff's vehicle before. It was kind of fun. All those gadgets on the dashboard."

For a second or two Kaylee was too stunned to answer. She and the sheriff exchanged glances. Did Gina really think she'd been summoned here for a pep talk?

"I'm sorry, Gina," Kaylee said. "We can't leave yet. Sheriff

Maddox needs to talk to you."

"There's more?"

The sheriff straightened a stack of papers on his desk, then leaned forward. The chair groaned as if to warn of bad news. At least that's how it seemed to Kaylee.

Gina's demeanor had changed during the conversation. Instead of a frightened bird who didn't know where to look, she appeared calm. Steady.

And totally unprepared for this shock.

"Maybe I should be the one," Kaylee blurted.

Sheriff Maddox gestured for her to go ahead.

Kaylee took a deep breath and faced Gina. "It's about Jake. He didn't die of a heart attack."

"He didn't?"

"I'm sorry, Gina. But the medical examiner in Seattle believes—that is, he suspects . . ." Kaylee paused to take another deep breath. "Well, it seems Jake was murdered."

The color fled from Gina's face. Before anyone could respond, she toppled out of her chair and hit the floor in a dead faint.

"This is all my fault." Kaylee paced in the hallway. "I should have found a better way to tell her."

"I've been doing this a long time," Sheriff Maddox said. "It's never easy."

"She just keeled over. Right there beside me. And I couldn't stop her. What if she had hit her head on your desk?"

"But she didn't. And you need to stop beating yourself up over this. No one could have expected her to react that way."

"Maybe we should have."

"Maybe. But it's over now. Are you going to be okay? Or are you going to pass out too?"

Though Kaylee appreciated the reassurance, she still felt the sting of causing Gina excruciating pain. She'd only wanted to help, and she thought Gina might prefer hearing such awful news from a friend instead of from the sheriff.

She couldn't have been more wrong.

After Gina regained consciousness and was checked for injuries, Sheriff Maddox had escorted Kaylee from the office. Aida and Nick stayed with Gina.

"Kaylee?" The sheriff's insistent tone pulled her from her self-recriminations. "Are you okay?"

"I'm fine. Just worried about Gina."

"Do you want me to have Nick drive you back to Turtle Cove? I can have one of the other deputies follow in your car."

"That won't be necessary. I'm fine, I promise."

Aida emerged from the office and beckoned to the sheriff. "Mrs. Beckett would like to see you. Both of you."

"Promise me something," Kaylee said quickly.

He raised an eyebrow in question.

"You do the talking."

The sheriff gave a wry smile. "Let's get this done so you ladies can go on home."

They returned to the office to find Gina sitting in her chair.

"Are you okay?" Kaylee asked quietly.

"Only a little woozy. I didn't mean to cause such a kerfuffle."

"I didn't mean to cause you to faint."

"I know." Gina grasped Kaylee's hand. "You're a good friend. Thank you for being here with me."

Kaylee simply nodded, then stood by the wall so Sheriff Maddox could sit in the chair next to Gina.

"I know this isn't easy," he said. "But I have to ask you a few questions."

"Do you think I killed my husband?"

"Did you?"

"Why would I kill Jake? I loved him. I still love him."

"Do you know if he had any enemies? Was he having trouble with anyone at the marina?"

Gina appeared to give the question serious thought while slowly shaking her head. "Not that I know of."

"Will you consent to a search?"

"Of Jake's office?"

"And your home." Sheriff Maddox said. "We never know where a piece of key evidence may be found. So we need to cover all our bases."

Gina's spine stiffened with indignation. "My parents always voted for you when they lived here."

"I, um, I appreciate that."

"People say you're a good man. And I think people are probably right."

"I appreciate that too."

"But I don't want to be the scapegoat."

"Mrs. Beckett," the sheriff began, but she held up her hand to stop him.

"Kaylee said you think my husband was murdered because of what you read in some report. But you haven't told me what's in the report. You haven't given me a copy."

"That's because you passed out. The report is right here on my desk."

"I would like a copy, please. And then I want to go home. Or are you arresting me?"

"Gina." Kaylee laid a placating hand on the younger woman's shoulder. "Sheriff Maddox doesn't arrest people without solid evidence. He only wants to find out who killed Jake."

"I've seen a lot of movies," Gina said. "And I know that the spouse is always the prime suspect in a murder investigation. I wouldn't be the first person on this island falsely accused of killing the man she loved."

Unfortunately, Gina was right. Kaylee understood the young woman's caution but was surprised by her uncharacteristic shrewdness. But where had this astuteness come from? Kaylee never would have expected Gina to stand up for herself like this. Why couldn't she be this strong all the time?

"Do I have your permission?" Sheriff Maddox asked. "We can come now, search both places, and call it a day."

"My copy of the report, please," Gina said firmly. It was a clear *no*.

Sheriff Maddox retrieved the document from his desk and handed it to Gina with his business card. "If you have any questions, call me."

"Thank you." Gina stood. "I don't really believe you'd railroad me or anything like that, Sheriff. But Jake's gone, and I have to watch out for myself. You understand, don't you?"

"I do, Mrs. Beckett. Like Kaylee said, I'm only after the person who killed your husband."

Gina straightened and lifted her chin. "I can assure you, Sheriff. That person was not me."

The sun was low in the sky when Kaylee and Gina left the sheriff's office. As soon as they climbed into the SUV, Kaylee called Mary to let her know she was on the way to The Flower Patch.

"Go ahead and lock up," she said after giving a brief update of the afternoon's events. "Bear will be fine until I get there."

"I'll wait for you," Mary answered. "Herb has a Youth Association meeting this evening so he's not pining for me to get home."

After ending the call, Kaylee glanced at Gina. "Do you want me to call Chad? I can tell him about Jake if you want me to."

"I'll call him later."

The confidence and poise she had demonstrated after her fainting spell was gone. That persona seemed to have sapped all her energy, and now she leaned her head back, eyes closed, clutching her bag with the copy of the medical examiner's report tucked safely inside.

"Is there anyone else? Your parents perhaps?"

Gina stared out the passenger window and mumbled something. Though Kaylee didn't catch her words, her body language definitely said *no.*

Neither of them spoke during the rest of the drive.

Once inside The Flower Patch, Kaylee and Gina joined Mary in the kitchen. The kettle whistled on the stove and scones from Jessica's bakery were on the table.

Bear jumped around Kaylee's legs, his tail wagging as fast as it could. She picked him up, holding his warm body beneath her chin. He licked her jaw as she scratched behind his ear. Her favorite pick-me-up.

"You two look done in," Mary said. "Come and sit."

While Gina sipped her tea and nibbled at a scone, Mary brought Kaylee up to date on customer orders and sales.

"Sylvia stopped in for you about an hour ago," she said.

"Did she say what she wanted?"

"Festivity Committee business. She's changed her mind about the town tree. Now she wants the Fraser fir."

"Why the change?"

"No idea. Just remember you get to make up your own mind. You don't have to go along with Sylvia if you don't want to."

"*Pseudotsuga menziesii* or *Abies fraseri*. They're both great options. But the *Pseudotsuga* is native to this area, so that's the one we should choose."

"I'm guessing that the *Pseudo*-whatever is the Douglas fir," Mary teased.

"Sorry," Kaylee said with a smile. "It's not actually a fir, thus the *pseudo* prefix. *Tsuga* is Greek for 'hemlock.' Botanists had so much trouble trying to classify it—it's like hemlock, firs, spruces, and pines, but also unlike each of them—that they changed its name over twenty times."

"And the rest of it?"

"Archibald Menzies is credited with documenting the tree so it's named for him. In 1791, I believe. The common name is after David Douglas, a rival botanist, who introduced it to his homeland of Scotland around 1827."

Gina made a huffing noise. "You really care about this stuff, don't you?"

"I do."

"Kaylee has a doctorate in plant taxonomy," Mary said.

"A doctorate? So why are you running a flower shop?"

"I used to teach at the University of Washington in Seattle," Kaylee said. "But I needed a change, so I bought my grandmother's business." It wasn't the whole truth, but she didn't like saying her position had been eliminated.

"I remember your grandmother," Gina said. "She provided the flowers for the homecoming court my senior year."

"Were you on the court, Gina?" Mary asked.

"Runner-up to the queen."

"Congratulations."

"It seemed so important then," Gina said. "But once you're

out of high school, none of that stuff matters. It hasn't even been that long ago, and you didn't know."

"I'm afraid I don't pay much attention to such things," Mary said.

"That's what I mean," Gina said. "After high school, other things matter. For most of a person's life, other things matter. Like having your own home. Your own family."

She paused to tear a corner from her scone but then crumbled it onto her plate. "Derek was my escort. He said he wanted to marry me. Then he changed his mind."

A tingle raced up Kaylee's spine. She and Mary exchanged glances, but neither of them spoke.

"It was like being runner-up on the homecoming court all over again." Gina tore another piece from her scone. "Then Derek died in that boating accident, and it all seemed so senseless. All our bickering and hurting one another. And now Jake is dead too." Her voice caught. "He's dead, murdered, and I don't know what to do without him."

Mary covered Gina's hand with her own. "I'm so very sorry. The whole thing must have come as quite a shock."

Gina focused her gaze on Mary. "I didn't do it."

"I didn't think you did."

Gina slowly turned to Kaylee. "What about you? Do you believe I'm innocent?"

"I do."

"I'm so tired, Kaylee."

"I'll take you home."

"I have a better idea," Mary said. "Gina, why don't you stay with me tonight? The guest room doesn't get used enough, and Herb won't be home until late."

"You're very kind, but I don't want to be any trouble."

"You'll be more trouble if you don't say yes."

"How's that?" Gina asked, puzzled.

"I won't sleep a wink all night from worrying about you."

"Really?"

"Really."

"Same here," Kaylee said. "You shouldn't be alone tonight. I'm only sorry I didn't think to offer."

"I just didn't realize . . . I didn't know." Gina tucked in her lower lip. "Thank you for caring. For believing me."

"We absolutely do," Mary said. "Just give me a few minutes to straighten up here and we'll be on our way."

"I'll clean up," Kaylee said. "It won't take a minute, and I want to go over tomorrow's orders before I head home."

"They're on your desk," Mary said. "See you in the morning."

After Mary and Gina left, Kaylee plopped into the easy chair in her office and pulled Bear onto her lap.

"I'm not sure I can go through this again, Bear. Another murder?" She shook her head in frustration. "I don't go looking for mysteries. But it sure seems like mysteries look for me."

14

"Rick Saunders has a girlfriend," Kaylee said to Mary after hanging up from talking to the talented artist who had painted a portrait of Bear. "He just ordered a dozen roses for her birthday."

"Must be serious. Anyone we know?"

"The new vet tech at Dr. Melody's. I met her when Bear got his heartworm shot. She seems really nice. Interesting though that Rick insisted on pink instead of red."

"Not quite ready to declare his undying love."

"Guess not." Kaylee retrieved the roses from the cooler to arrange Rick's order. "You know, this is the first time this week I've been in the shop the entire day. No appointments. No hunting for clues. No more crazy encounters with Whitney."

"I hope you didn't just jinx yourself," Mary teased.

"Me too."

"I don't think you have to worry about Whitney, though. Herb called while you were on the phone with Rick. She was with her film crew at the diner for lunch. He overheard them talking about the Northern Lights Inn and the Turtleback Country Club."

"Fancy places, huh?"

"They need promoting too."

"Speaking of Whitney, have you heard from Gina?" Kaylee artfully arranged the dozen roses and greenery in a full-bodied glass vase. Then she began to go through their collection of ribbons for the perfect one to tie around the vase. Rick had done a great job on Bear's portrait so she wanted to go above and beyond on his order.

"No, but I imagine she's worn out from subbing today," Mary said. "Probably a blessing she got called in."

"At least she didn't have time to brood over Jake," Kaylee said. "Or those clues."

"She showed me the last one after we got home yesterday. I wish I knew what it meant."

"I imagine only one person does. I'm convinced Whitney and Jake had a history."

"Well, if we can't figure out the clue, and Whitney never sees it, the search will be over. Maybe that's for the best. At least for Gina."

Their conversation turned to other topics as they filled additional orders and waited on customers. A couple of off-islanders, in town for the day, fell in love with DeeDee's collection of lavender products. One of the women adored Mary's one-of-a-kind peppermint-studded wreath, which prompted her friend to ask for a custom-designed wreath of her own. While Mary talked with her about possibilities and rang up their orders, Kaylee put the finishing touches on Rick's birthday roses.

She loved days like this: talking with customers, breathing in the fragrance of a variety of flowers, creating something beautiful for a special occasion. As soon as the women left, she'd deliver the flowers to Rick's girlfriend.

The phone rang just as she stuck the card pick into the vase.

"Good afternoon. This is The Flower Patch."

"Kaylee? Is that you?" The voice was wobbly.

"Gina? What's wrong?"

"Someone broke into my house. They're gone."

"What's gone?"

"Please come over. You're the only one who understands."

Kaylee wasn't sure about that, but it didn't matter.

Somehow Gina had become her responsibility, like a stray kitten in need of care.

"Have you called the sheriff's office?" Kaylee asked.

"I called *you*. Will you come?" she pleaded.

"Are you sure whoever broke into the house isn't still there? Are you safe?"

"I looked everywhere." A note of pride crept into Gina's tone. "Even under the beds and in the closets."

"What would you have done if you found somebody?"

"Scream," she said as if the answer was obvious.

Kaylee rubbed her temple where a Gina-induced ache now throbbed.

"I have a delivery to make but it's on the way." Maybe not exactly on the way, but the detour wouldn't take long. "I'll be there soon."

"Thanks, Kaylee. I knew I could count on you."

"Just don't touch anything, okay? The sheriff may want to check for prints."

"Won't my prints already be everywhere? I mean, I live here and I touch things all the time."

"But we don't want to mess up any new prints, right?"

"Got it. I'll wait for you out front."

Kaylee started to object. The outdoor temperature was only just above freezing. But what was the use? If Gina got too cold she'd surely have the sense to go back inside.

At least Kaylee hoped she would.

The house, a compact two-bedroom on a narrow street of similar houses, exuded cozy hospitality. The furniture in the front room was a pleasant mix of upholstery and polished wood, making a comfortable room to relax in, to entertain friends, to simply be.

Not at all what Kaylee had expected, considering Gina's unpredictable personality.

"This is lovely," she said.

"Do you think so?" Gina asked.

"I do."

"Jake made the tables and the entertainment unit." A flush of pink touched her cheeks. "But I designed them. It's fun to decorate."

"You have a talent for it."

"Thanks, Kaylee. That means a lot coming from you."

"Why from me?"

"Because you have talent too. Everyone talks about your flowers. So if you think this—" she gestured around the room "—is good, then maybe it is."

"Believe me, Gina." Kaylee put as much reassurance in her voice as possible. "It is very good. But that's not why I'm here."

"The clues." Gina opened the lid on a narrow rolltop desk. "I had put Jake's letter and the tin we found at the landing here. Now they're gone."

"Are you sure that's where you left them? Maybe you misplaced them."

"I've searched everywhere. In my dresser, in the kitchen. But face it, Kaylee. This place isn't that big and there aren't that many hiding spots. They're gone."

"Is anything else missing?"

"Not that I can see. At least I still have the clue you found at the barreling plant."

"It doesn't make any sense," Kaylee said. "Why would anyone want those other clues?"

Though perhaps—oh, surely not. Kaylee might not like Whitney very much, but that didn't mean she should suspect her of theft.

"Do we have to call the police?" Gina asked. "I'm not sure I want to. Sheriff Maddox suspects me—"

"He never said that."

"He didn't have to. Though when you think about it, this theft proves I'm innocent. Would you like something? Tea? Coffee?"

"Coffee," Kaylee said firmly, her mind in a whirl as she tried to puzzle out Gina's logic. "Strong coffee."

A spontaneous grin brightened Gina's face. "One cup of strong coffee coming up. Will you call the sheriff? He likes you more than me."

Before Kaylee could respond, Gina left the room. Kaylee perched on the edge of an easy chair and pulled out her phone.

"Hi, Aida," she said. "This is Kaylee Bleu. Could I talk to the sheriff please?"

After ending the call, Kaylee joined Gina in the kitchen and was struck again with the young woman's decorating skill. The room, a tastefully sunny square with a table tucked into a corner, had a nautical motif. The theme was common on the island, but Gina had focused on yellows and greens instead of the typical blues and reds. Pops of deep purple added her own original touch.

"The sheriff will be here soon," Kaylee said as she took a seat. "This room is lovely too. I like your color combination."

Four grayscale prints in thick wooden frames decorated a wall behind the table. Each one showed the same scene of the harbor, including the Old Cape Lighthouse, during a different season.

"These are interesting," Kaylee continued. "I've never seen anything like them in the tourist shops."

"I found the original photos in albums that belonged to my grandparents. They had dozens of them, but these four are my favorite. My grandfather took each one from the same spot on the other side of West Sound. At least that's the story I was told."

She placed a carousel of assorted coffee blends in front of Kaylee. "I had them enlarged and Jake made the frames out of reclaimed wood. He was so talented."

Kaylee selected a pod and handed it to Gina. "It sounds like you were close to your grandparents."

"As much as I could be. They wanted to raise Chad and me. Even tried to get custody a couple of times when Mom and Dad separated. But then our parents would reconcile and forbid any contact with our grandparents. It got tiresome."

"I'm so sorry, Gina." Kaylee's own childhood had been so idyllic, she had once assumed everyone else's had been the same way. But as she entered her adult years, she'd discovered that happy childhoods were rare. Her heart always ached for those who hadn't had the kind of childhood she felt everyone deserved.

"It wasn't an easy way to live," Gina said as hot coffee poured from the machine's spout into a mug. "And when my grandparents died, I felt like I had died too."

"How old were you?"

"Thirteen. They were killed in a car accident while on vacation in San Diego." Gina set the mug in front of Kaylee, then pulled her legs up to sit cross-legged in the opposite chair. "I was supposed to go with them, but I backed out at the last minute. A friend asked me to spend the weekend sailing with her family. That sounded like more fun."

It wasn't hard to see where this was going. No wonder Gina was such a mess. A difficult family life and at least three horrific tragedies—first her grandparents, then her boyfriend, and now her husband.

"It wasn't your fault they died."

"I know that." Gina's voice was barely audible. "But I can't help but wonder if things would have been different if I'd been there. It's like that butterfly effect. If I had gone, would they have been on that road at that moment?"

"Nobody can know that," Kaylee said kindly. "We can't change the past no matter how much we might want to."

"So what are we supposed to do when the past is so hard?"

"Learn from it."

"What was I supposed to learn?"

"You still have a future, Gina. It's up to you how you prepare for it."

"I'm afraid I'll make a mistake."

"We're all afraid sometimes." Kaylee gave her a gentle smile. "I was so scared when I first moved here. I'd been teaching at the university for so long. It was my life. To come here and become a business owner was scary."

"But it wasn't a mistake."

"I know that now, but I couldn't have at the time. The point is we never know for sure how things will turn out. It's possible the accident still would have happened."

Kaylee didn't say the obvious. She knew that Gina had struggled, probably still struggled, with the alternate possibilities since her grandparents died. Perhaps the accident wouldn't have happened if Gina had been with them. They might not have been at that particular place at that particular time. But what if they had? Then Gina might have died too.

Kaylee wasn't a psychologist or therapist, but after years of working with students from all kinds of backgrounds, she'd picked up a smattering of insight. She had no doubt that Gina was eaten up with guilt that her beloved grandparents—and boyfriend, and husband—had died and she hadn't.

When the doorbell rang, both women returned to the living room. Sheriff Maddox entered along with Deputy Robyn Garcia. As usual, Robyn's light-brown hair was pulled back into a ponytail.

She scanned the living room before she greeted Kaylee and Gina. Kaylee guessed that Robyn was as surprised as she had been by its cozy charm.

Gina pointed to the desk and told her story.

"When I got home from teaching, I went to the desk to write a check to Chad. He'd bought a part for my car. That's when I realized the clues were missing."

"Is there any possibility you put them someplace else?" Sheriff Maddox asked.

"I looked every other place I might have put them, even though I *know* I left them in the desk. Right there in that cubbyhole. The tin box barely fit."

"Any ideas on who might have wanted them?"

"None."

"What about you?" The sheriff turned to Kaylee. "Any suspects?"

"Not really."

"That's not very convincing."

She couldn't exactly tell the sheriff that she suspected Gina's late husband had left this trail for another woman, especially with the fragile Gina standing right there. "The notes and flowers are only important to the person meant to find them," she said truthfully.

"Hmm." Hands on his waist, the sheriff bent to peer into the desk's cubbyholes. "Deputy Garcia, could you dust for prints, please? The door too, though I don't think it was forced open."

"They probably came through the back door," Gina said. "I never lock it."

"Why not?"

"Because this is Turtle Cove. Nothing ever happens here."

"Dust the back door too, please," Sheriff Maddox said to Robyn.

She nodded and snapped on plastic gloves she pulled from her pocket.

"Anything else missing?" the sheriff asked Gina.

"Nothing."

"Not much to go on, is there?" He peered around the room again as if he could find the name of the thief hidden somewhere on the dusky blue walls.

"At least it proves I didn't kill my husband."

The sheriff's head snapped toward Gina so quickly Kaylee half expected it to fall off his neck.

"How does it prove that?" he said.

"It's obvious, isn't it? Someone wants to hurt me, maybe even frame me for Jake's—for what happened to Jake. Whoever did that stole the clues too. They must have."

"Interesting theory."

"At least I still have the last clue, the one Kaylee found at Shortcake's. I had it with me. In my bag."

"Can I see it?"

Gina retrieved the box. "The tin that was stolen was identical to this one."

The sheriff snapped photos of the tin, then made notes while Gina described the pressed flowers and stationery.

"After Deputy Garcia finishes here, she'll talk to a few neighbors. Find out if anyone saw anything. I'm afraid that's about all we can do for now. But please feel free to call if you think of anything else."

"Thanks, Sheriff. I'm glad you don't suspect me anymore."

Instead of answering, he smiled a humorless smile. Kaylee wasn't sure Gina's theory had convinced the sheriff of her innocence. In fact, her logic—or lack thereof—had probably suggested a new theory to him.

"I'll be going now," he said. "Kaylee, a word?"

It wasn't really a request. Kaylee grabbed her coat and followed the sheriff to his car. Robyn's car was parked behind his.

"Who's the thief?"

"You think I know?"

"I think you have a pretty good idea. And I think I do too."

"You think Gina pretended the clues were stolen to deflect suspicion that she murdered Jake."

"Can you blame me? No signs of forced entry. Nothing of any real value taken. Who cares about a couple crushed flowers?"

"They were pressed flowers."

"What?"

"Pressed flowers. Not crushed flowers."

"What's the difference?" He held up a hand. "Don't answer that. I don't really want to know."

"Gina may have faked the robbery," Kaylee admitted. "But I don't believe for a moment that she killed her husband. There's absolutely no motive—"

"That we know of."

"That fainting spell in your office was no act. She was stunned."

"Stunned we found out the truth. What about big insurance payout?"

"I'll never believe it. Her grief is real."

"You have any alternate theories?"

"Perhaps it was something to do with Jake's business," Kaylee said. "Or maybe he had a secret gambling problem."

"We're checking into those possibilities. But until we find something to indicate otherwise, Gina Beckett is my number-one suspect."

There was nothing else for it. She'd have to come clean. "There may be someone else."

He raised an eyebrow. "Who?"

"Whitney Mills."

"You mean the gal wandering all over the island with the camera guys?"

"She's very interested in the clues. Too interested. I think she and Jake might have been . . . involved a few years ago. Her family vacationed here once."

"That's why her name's familiar. I remember now. That was the summer the Glasser boy died. I flew to Olympia to get her statement."

"A statement from Whitney? Why?"

He appeared thoughtful. "You're right about her and Jake. It's all coming back now. There were rumors of a romantic triangle going on. Like she was playing Jake and Derek against each other."

"I thought Derek was Gina's boyfriend."

"So maybe there was more than one romantic triangle. Didn't matter. It was a wasted trip. Miss Mills didn't know anything, and she denied having any kind of relationship with Derek." He rubbed the back of his neck. "I must be getting old not to have placed her sooner. Maybe I should look into retirement. Let someone else take over this job."

"You don't mean that."

"No I don't. But it sure would be nice to have more time to spend with that grandbaby."

Just the thought of the new little girl in his life caused the sheriff to smile from ear to ear. Kaylee couldn't help but smile too.

"I'm sure it would be," she said. "But we still need you here."

After he drove away, Kaylee returned to the house. Robyn was putting away her printing kit while Gina cleaned the powder from the oak desk.

"Find anything?" Kaylee asked.

"A few good prints. Let's hope they don't all belong to Gina."

"They will," Gina said.

"What makes you think so?" Robyn asked.

"Because thieves wear gloves. Everybody knows that."

"You'd be surprised how dumb criminals can be." Robyn closed the clasps on her kit and gripped the handle.

"Not this one. He almost got away with killing Jake, didn't he?"

"He?" Robyn asked.

"He, she, whoever." Gina sounded exasperated. "The point is we're dealing with a criminal mastermind who murdered my husband and stole my private property in broad daylight."

"I'm going to interview your neighbors right now," Robyn said soothingly. "I can promise you, Mrs. Beckett, we'll do our best to find out who's responsible."

Gina nodded as her eyes shimmered with tears. "I'd like to be alone now."

"Are you sure?" Kaylee asked. "I don't mind staying."

"I need to be at the marina early in the morning. I'll be fine, I promise."

Kaylee glanced at Robyn.

"I'll arrange drive-bys," Robyn said. "Remember to lock your doors and windows."

"I promise." Gina's voice wavered, and she folded her arms against her stomach. "I need some time by myself."

"We'll go then," Kaylee said with reluctance. "But please call me if you need anything."

"Thanks, Kaylee. I will. Thank you too, Deputy Garcia. It was nice to meet you."

Gina closed the door after them, and Kaylee and Robyn walked together to their cars.

"She's an odd one, isn't she?" Robyn said conversationally.

"A little bit. I hate leaving her like this."

"Don't worry. We'll keep a close watch on her." Robyn opened her trunk and placed the printing kit inside. "Gina showed me the remaining clue while you were out with the sheriff. Any idea what it means?"

"I wish. But it's too obscure."

"Wonder why Jake made the clues so hard. It's almost like he didn't want her to follow them."

Maybe because they were never meant for Gina.

It was past time for Kaylee to have another talk with Whitney.

15

Kaylee parked her SUV and walked up the porch stairs at the back of the mansion. Once again, she almost tripped over the loose board. With everything else that had been going on, she'd totally forgotten to call Reese to fix it. Funny that she hadn't seen him around town lately. Though he was probably as busy as she was. Several of the elderly island residents counted on him to help them with their exterior Christmas lights. Add that to his regular handyman calls and he probably didn't have time even for a coffee break at the bakery or to stop in at The Flower Patch for a bit of small-town gossip.

Bear ran to greet her, his toenails scrabbling on the wood floor, as she entered. She scooped him up and kissed the top of his head. "I've been leaving you alone too much lately, haven't I? It's a good thing Mary likes you almost as much as I do."

Muffled voices and laughter came from the workroom so she headed for that part of the house.

"Oh good. You're back," Mary said as she entered. DeeDee and Jessica perched on tall stools and all three were placing carnations in an assortment of different-size mason jars.

"What's going on?"

"Last-minute order from Sylvia. She and Penelope are having a party this evening and they need these in less than an hour. So I called in the troops."

"That's odd. Sylvia is usually so organized."

"Sylvia thought Penelope had placed the order, and Penelope thought Sylvia had. It wasn't until they both came in here to pick up the flowers that we discovered there was no order." Mary glued a rosette to a ribbon and fastened it around the neck of a jar. "Pull up a seat and give us a hand."

"Yes ma'am. I wish I had been here to see that mix-up."

"Can't you just imagine it?" DeeDee said. "'Why, Penelope, I'm certain as can be it was your turn to order the flowers.'" Her exaggerated Southern drawl was spot-on. "'How can that be, sister? You know good and well I ordered the flowers the last time.'"

They all laughed, then Kaylee told them about her visit with Gina. Soon the arrangements were finished and divided into four boxes. Each woman carried a box across the street to The Chandlery Gift Shop.

Sylvia and Penelope thanked Kaylee for filling their order so quickly.

"And these are lovely, dear. You do come up with the most imaginative ideas."

"The thanks go to Mary," Kaylee said. Penelope's cat, Peaches, sprawled on a nearby buffet table as if she didn't have a care in the world. Kaylee stifled a giggle. "I got in on the tail end of this project."

She turned to pet the cat as another giggle threatened to erupt. The other women chatted a few more minutes, but the sisters were in a hurry to get home and make sure everything was ready for their guests. Soon the Petal Pushers were back out on Main Street.

DeeDee glanced at her watch. "A little after six. Guess we can all lock up."

"And then what?" Jessica asked. "Luke is out of town, and I've got the whole evening ahead of me. Let's do something."

"Like what?" DeeDee chuckled. "Toilet-paper the lighthouse?"

"Do kids still do that?" Mary asked then gazed off as if skipping down memory lane. "Those were the days."

"You never!" Jessica feigned shock.

"Maybe once or twice." Mary winked.

"We should make plans," DeeDee said. "Andy and the girls can have an impromptu father/daughter night. It's been awhile since they've done that."

"What about you, Kaylee?" Mary asked. "You in?"

"I am so in," she said. "Dinner at O'Brien's?"

The other three chorused agreement, then laughed.

"I'll drive," DeeDee volunteered. "Let's meet at the van in, say, twenty minutes?"

"Actually, I'll meet you at the restaurant," Kaylee said. "It's too cold to eat outside on the patio so I'm going to take Bear home first."

Kaylee and Mary went inside the mansion while Jessica and DeeDee walked toward the bakery and the bookstore.

"This is fun," Mary said. "I love it when we're able to do spur-of-the-moment things."

"Me too." Kaylee maneuvered Bear's winter coat over his body and fastened the straps.

"You go ahead," Mary said. "I can finish closing up. We'll see you at the restaurant."

"Don't wait on me to get a table. I won't be too far behind you."

"See you there."

Kaylee cradled Bear in one arm and grabbed her large tote with the other. As she headed out the back door, she reminded herself to be careful on the step, then placed Bear inside her SUV. She slid into the driver's side. Something was stuck under her windshield wiper.

Though curious, she started the ignition to get the heater running then slid out to retrieve the paper. Back inside, she left the door open to keep the interior light on and read the outside of the envelope. The letters K-A-L-Y were written on it in block letters.

"You think that means me, Bear?"

She opened the envelope and slid out a folded piece of notebook paper. "Fancy stationery," she muttered as she unfolded it.

The childish writing matched that on the envelope. Whoever had written the note obviously wanted to disguise his or her handwriting, and wasn't a good speller.

Busybodys only cause trouble. So you better stop. Or else.

TROUBLE!!!

Kaylee read the note again then peered through each of her windows. The sun had set, and the street lamps shone only circles of light. But here, in the small parking area behind the mansion, the area was well lit. No one was near the SUV.

Was someone lurking in the shadows?

Someone who knew she had returned to The Flower Patch. Who had waited until she'd gone inside and then slipped the note under her windshield wiper.

Was that person watching now? Waiting to see what she would do?

She swallowed the rising panic, then shut and locked her door so the interior light turned off. Mary was still inside The Flower Patch. Jessica was next door at her bakery, and DeeDee was just down the street at her bookstore.

If someone *was* watching, would they threaten her? Would they harm her friends?

She could be overreacting. After all, this wasn't the first anonymous note she'd received since moving to Turtle Cove.

That was it. She *was* overreacting.

But with an open murder investigation, albeit a quiet one

since Sheriff Maddox had managed to keep the results of the medical examiner's report out of the press, Kaylee couldn't take a chance of risking her safety or that of her friends.

She pulled out her phone and called Mary.

"I'm sure it's nothing," she said when Mary answered. "But I found a note on my windshield. It's slightly threatening."

"Where are you?" Mary asked in alarm.

"Still parked outside. I want to be sure you, DeeDee, and Jessica are okay in case whoever wrote this note is still hanging around."

Ever practical, Mary immediately took charge. "Stay where you are. I'll be out in a moment."

"I'm going to call Robyn Garcia. If she's still around, maybe she can check the note for prints."

Robyn answered right away. Kaylee told her what happened, and they agreed to meet at the bakery. A moment later Mary slid into the SUV's passenger seat, much to Bear's delight.

"Robyn is on her way," Kaylee said. "She'll meet us at Jessica's."

"Let me see the note."

"I need to put it in a plastic bag first. Can you reach that crate behind my seat? There's a box of ziplock bags inside."

Mary retrieved the box. "Do you always carry these around?"

"Doesn't everyone?" Kaylee teased. "Seriously, I never know when I'm going to find an interesting plant."

"Or possible evidence in a murder case."

"That too." Kaylee slipped the note and envelope into a clear bag then put the car in reverse. "I'm going to pull around and park on Main Street."

"I'll text Jess and DeeDee to let them know."

As Kaylee pulled to a stop in front of the bakery, Jessica opened the door and waved for them to come inside. DeeDee was already there.

They gathered around the counter so DeeDee and Jessica could read the note through the bag.

"What in the world does it mean?" DeeDee asked.

Mary turned from peering out the front window. "My guess is somebody wants Kaylee to stop helping Gina with the clues."

"In that case, they needn't have bothered," Kaylee said. "I don't have any idea where that clue leads. And Gina doesn't either."

"It's so juvenile," Jessica said. "I understand disguising the writing. I certainly would if I was going to write an anonymous note. But the wording seems purposely childish. As if the person is trying to appear uneducated."

"I agree," DeeDee said. "Whoever wrote this isn't as dumb as they want you to think."

Kaylee thought about what Gina said earlier—that whoever killed Jake was a criminal mastermind. But how could the trail Jake had created have anything to do with his murder? She didn't see how the treasure hunt and Jake's death could be related.

If Jake was trying to hide something from somebody, then why create a trail at all? If he was hiding something he wanted Gina to find in case he died, then why make the clues so cryptic she couldn't solve them? If the trail was meant for Whitney, then Jake had probably created the trail years ago. How then could it have anything to do with his death?

"This changes our plans," Jessica said. "But not the fact that I'm hungry. We should get something delivered so we're here when Robyn gets here. Pizza or Chinese?"

By the time the food was delivered, both a pizza and an assortment of Chinese cartons, Robyn had arrived and concluded that there were no prints on the note. She and Kaylee had also investigated the graveled parking area behind The Flower Patch but couldn't find anything helpful.

At their invitation, Robyn joined them for supper. Jessica provided beverages and desserts, and the conversation ran the gamut of small-town topics. Kaylee joined in, but a corner of her mind was preoccupied with the note, the unsolved clue, and Jake's death.

Removing the murder from the equation, she could only think of two people who might have written the note.

First thing tomorrow, she planned to have a chat with her primary suspect.

16

Robyn had taken the note with her to give to the sheriff when the impromptu get-together at the bakery ended last night. But Jessica had made a copy of it for Kaylee.

She went over it now, then peered through her windshield at the mechanic's shop. Chad's truck was parked off to the side. Since it wasn't quite eight in the morning, she hadn't been sure he would be there yet.

On her drive over, she'd rehearsed what to say, but now her carefully planned script seemed ridiculous. Confronting someone in her imagination was much different than doing so in real life.

But she had to do this.

Her mind made up, she strode into the open door of the auto bay, stopping inside the entrance to allow her eyes to adjust to the difference in the lighting. The acrid odor of grease and oil assaulted her nostrils.

"Kaylee?" a voice called. "Is that you?"

Kaylee forced a smile as Chad came her way, wiping his hands on a large cloth. "Hi, Chad."

"Something wrong with your vehicle?" He gave a good-natured grin.

This was the most relaxed and natural, Kaylee had ever seen him. Perhaps it had something to do with the garage. She often felt most herself at The Flower Patch. The only place that meant more to her was Wildflower Cottage. Sometimes she still had to pinch herself to know she wasn't dreaming. Her grandparents' beloved home was now hers. She never wanted to live anywhere else.

Maybe this garage was where Chad felt most at home. Unfortunately, she was about to upset his good mood. It wasn't something she wanted to do. But what choice did she have?

As if he'd heard her question, she could hear Sheriff Maddox's voice echo in her head. *You should be letting me take care of this.*

Except she couldn't. If Chad hadn't sent the note, then why cause him the aggravation of being questioned by the sheriff or one of his deputies?

"You need a tune-up or is something else wrong?" he asked, his voice bringing her back to the conversation.

"Nothing like that," Kaylee said. "Someone left a note on my windshield last night. Here's a copy."

She focused intently on Chad's expression as he took the note and read it. No guilt showed on his face, only confusion and then a flare of anger.

"Who did this?" he demanded.

"No idea. Deputy Garcia checked it for prints but there weren't any."

"She has the original?"

"It's evidence."

He scanned the note again. "I don't understand why anyone would—I mean, who cares about those silly clues except for Gina?"

Then his eyes widened slightly as if he'd just realized something.

Kaylee stopped herself from asking, knowing he wouldn't tell her. Maybe he didn't have to.

"You didn't write it." She made it a statement, not a question.

"Did you think I did? Is that why you're here?"

"You asked me not to go with Gina to find the first cache. Remember?"

"So I did." He returned the note to her. "Why would I need to do something like this then?"

"Because I went with her anyway."

"You don't like me much, do you?"

"I hardly know you." Kaylee folded the sheet of paper and stuffed it in her bag. "But I saw how you handled things at Jake's funeral. It's obvious you care about your sister very much."

"I didn't realize you were watching."

"Not watching. Just noticing."

"I didn't send the note. In fact, I'd like to know what Jake hid away at the end of his little trail."

"We seem to be stuck on the latest clue."

"So I've heard."

Kaylee glanced around the garage while she gathered her thoughts. She was convinced Chad suspected who had sent the note. But would he tell her? There was only one way to find out. "You weren't my only suspect." She met his gaze and held it. "I think someone else is interested in this."

"Anyone I know?"

"You tell me."

He didn't say anything, but Kaylee sensed he was evaluating her as he considered his answer.

"I meant what I said," Chad finally replied. "I'd like to know where the clues lead. But I'm not sure I want Gina to know."

"Because you think the trail was meant for someone else?"

He pressed his lips together and nodded.

"I think so too."

"Whitney didn't want her family to know about Jake. They wouldn't have approved. But they couldn't keep it a secret from everyone. Jake was mad-dog crazy about her."

"But he married Gina."

"She was mad-dog crazy about him."

Kaylee thought about the sheriff's suggestion that there had been a couple of romantic triangles going on that summer.

Both Whitney and Gina were interested in Jake. Both Jake and Gina's boyfriend, Derek, were interested in Whitney.

Then Derek died, Whitney left the island with her family, and the two remaining characters in the summer drama—Gina and Jake—married each other.

"Were you and Derek good friends?"

"Did Gina tell you about him?"

"A little." And so had Sheriff Maddox, but Chad didn't need to know that.

"I'm surprised. She seemed to close that book when she and Jake got engaged."

Kaylee wasn't sure, but a tinge of bitterness seemed to creep into his voice. But maybe that was her imagination.

"Why don't you let me talk to Gina about that note?" Chad suggested. "She gets some strange ideas sometimes, but I'm sure she didn't mean to frighten you."

"Wait a minute." Kaylee shook her head in confusion. "You think Gina wrote that note?"

"Don't you?"

"No. Why would she?" But what if Gina had? If Sheriff Maddox's suspicion that Gina had staged the break-in was right, then Chad could be right about this. Considering Gina's roller-coaster personality, it wasn't that far-fetched an idea.

"I'm sure in her mind it made sense. Maybe she doesn't want to follow the clues anymore but didn't want to admit that to you." A smile softened his expression. "You've made an impression on her," he said. "She wouldn't want to disappoint you."

"Disappoint me? Why would I—?" Kaylee gave up. Chad was right about Gina. Look how she had twisted things in her mind with her criminal mastermind theory. Did Chad know about that? Did he even know that Jake had been murdered?

"I wouldn't be surprised if she was the one who 'stole'

those clues either," Chad said. "I don't want to say anything negative about my sister. I love her, and we're all each other has now that Jake's gone. But like I said, she has a strange way of thinking about things sometimes."

"I never suspected Gina," Kaylee admitted.

"You suspect Whitney?"

"It doesn't matter. I guess I should get to work. And let you get back to yours."

"I'm glad you stopped by. I just hope you believe me about that note. It's not from me."

"I do. Thanks."

Kaylee was almost to her SUV when Chad called after her. She turned, and he hurried toward her.

"What is it?" she asked.

"I have a favor to ask, but I'm not sure you'll like it."

"I have to hear it first."

"If you solve that clue, could we keep Gina out of it?"

Kaylee opened her mouth, but no words came out. How could she agree to something like that?

"I know what you're thinking, but look at it like this. If Jake created the trail for Whitney, and Gina finds out, she'll be devastated. It'll be like losing him all over again. But if you and I can figure out where the trail leads, then we'll know who it was for. If it's for Gina, we can leave the cache where it is and take her to it. But if not, then Gina never needs to know."

"I'm not sure I can agree to that."

"There's another reason. What if the clues and Jake's murder are connected?"

So he did know the truth about Jake's death. She shouldn't be surprised. Gina would certainly have confided in her brother. "I suppose they could be."

"By following the trail, maybe we can figure out what

happened. Wouldn't that be the best way to help Gina?"

"Perhaps," Kaylee said doubtfully.

"I understand your hesitation. But think about it, okay? That's all I ask."

Kaylee nodded then continued to her vehicle. What Chad said made sense. But to hunt for the clues without Gina's knowledge seemed like a betrayal.

At least for now, the dilemma was moot. No one seemed to know the answer to Jake's latest clue. Until someone did, Kaylee didn't have to choose between potential heartache and disloyalty.

And if Chad was right, and no one figured out the clue, Jake's murder might never be solved.

As difficult as it was, Kaylee decided to wait to talk to Whitney until after the stroll down Main Street had been filmed. The crew arrived a few moments early, and Whitney swept into The Flower Patch ready to direct the action with all the efficiency and poise of a queen bee instructing her drones. With the assistance of two deputies, one at each end, the street was closed to traffic.

Jessica's stand of cocoa and baked goods was set up in front of her decorated window, and she wore a thick white sweater with glistening green and red threads shimmering through the weave. A matching beret perched on her straight, black hair.

"You look lovely," Kaylee said while Whitney set up the initial establishing shot of the Victorian mansion. "What a cute outfit."

"Isn't it though? Whitney chose it for me." Jessica's dark eyes sparkled with mischief. "Do you think I could convince her to do all my clothes shopping?"

"She has good taste. You should at least try."

DeeDee joined them, and Whitney appeared to brief them on their roles. Kaylee returned to The Flower Patch while DeeDee stayed near the bakery with Jessica. After a couple of walk-throughs, the camera crew prepared to film.

On Whitney's cue, Kaylee emerged from The Flower Patch and waved. Then she joined her friends and accepted a cup of cocoa from Jessica. Now it was DeeDee's turn. While the camera rolled, she strolled past High Tide Outfitters, stopping a moment for its owner to have the spotlight, then she crossed the street. When she reached her bookstore, DeeDee greeted Sylvia and Penelope. The camera switched to follow the two sisters past The Chic Boutique to their gift shop.

The stroll continued up the next block with other shop owners taking turns leading the camera. They crossed Main Street again and returned to The Flower Patch. Before the camera arrived, all the owners were in their Whitney-directed places on the mansion's large veranda to shout "Happy Holidays!" in unison.

When the filming ended, Kaylee expected Whitney to find fault with the amateur actors. But Whitney told them what a great job they'd done and made a point to especially comment on a couple of the interactions.

"We have to do it at least two more times just to be sure we have enough great footage to splice together. But you all are terrific. I can't tell you how much it means to me that you're willing to work so hard for this promo."

"Anything to bring in more winter tourists," said Vince Mack, the owner of High Tide Outfitters. "We've got all the gear they need for fun in the snow or on the water. And if we don't, we'll get it."

Once the filming was finished, Jessica handed out cups of cocoa to the crew. Whitney joined the other retailers on the mansion's veranda to thank them again for their cooperation. Kaylee stayed on the fringes, eager for the chance to talk to Whitney in private while also dreading it.

Before long, she realized Whitney was also purposely sticking around. Nora Keller, the talented owner of the Art Attack, was the last to leave the veranda. Whitney had commandeered a couple of Native American sculptures to include in a separate promo spot designed to attract the artistic crowd. Nora seemed especially pleased by the well-deserved attention. Kaylee was happy for her.

And mystified by Whitney.

Her behavior at Shortcake Bistro had seemed insincere. Kaylee was sure Whitney hadn't been nearly as interested in the gallery as she pretended to be.

But her interest in Nora's work certainly appeared genuine.

As she reconsidered her opinion of Whitney, Kaylee had to admit she might have been unfair. Her animosity centered around Whitney's attitude toward Gina and her nosy interest in Jake's trail. But if Whitney also believed the trail was meant for her, then of course she'd be interested. Kaylee couldn't fault her for that.

In fact, if Whitney had arrived at the island before Gina roped Kaylee into helping her with Jake's clues, perhaps Kaylee and Whitney would have become friends. Maybe not best buddies, but Kaylee certainly would have invited her to supper some evening.

She and Jessica had already decided to take another stab at going to O'Brien's this evening.

Perhaps it wasn't too late to include Whitney.

Though that depended on how their conversation about the anonymous note turned out.

After Nora took her leave, Whitney smiled at Kaylee. "I think that was a success. Thanks again for making sure the window displays are so festive and beautiful."

"I didn't do much."

"But what you did made a difference. I doubt the insurance agent down the street would have had anything other than a wreath in his window if not for you."

Kaylee grinned. "That's probably true. He's a bit of a minimalist."

"Or he'd rather be anywhere else than in his office. I don't know how he runs a business without any administrative help."

"His wife used to take care of all that for him. After she died, I guess he didn't want anyone else coming in. Besides, I'm not sure how much business he actually does anymore. Files a claim here and there, but he's practically retired."

"Anyway, I just wanted you to know that I noticed. And I appreciate your help."

"I enjoyed it. I think we're all excited about being part of an actual television commercial."

"Most of it will end up on the cutting room floor, I'm afraid. It took several minutes to make that trek up and down the block. Commercials only last a few seconds."

"Then why go to all the trouble?"

"To engage people. To make them feel good and welcome." Whitney leaned against a railing, her demeanor relaxed and content. "The art department will pull out the best clips and create a montage that begins and ends with this lovely mansion. Other clips may be included with other things we've filmed. Then there are the stills. We certainly have lots of material to work from."

"Does that mean you're finished filming?"

"The crew is leaving this afternoon."

"What about you?"

"I'm not ready to go yet."

This was the right time to invite Whitney to dinner. But Kaylee couldn't do that until she'd asked about the note. She pulled the paper from her pocket and held it out to Whitney.

"Someone put this on my windshield last night."

Whitney glanced at her in puzzlement, then unfolded the note just as Chad had earlier that morning.

But the moment quickly ended as two red blotches appeared on Whitney's cheeks.

"Is this a copy? Where's the original?"

"The sheriff has it."

"You called the sheriff?"

"I called one of his deputies. She checked it for prints."

The blotches grew even larger. "Did she find any?"

"Only smudges."

Whitney shook the paper at Kaylee, her body rigid. "You think I did this?"

"I don't know who did it."

"Well, it wasn't me." Whitney tore the paper into pieces and threw them down on the porch, then paced back and forth along the veranda in an obvious attempt to calm herself down.

Kaylee stood quietly against one of the porch columns. She wasn't sure how she had expected Whitney to react, but it certainly hadn't been like this.

"I didn't mean to upset you," Kaylee said quietly. "I just want to know who wrote the note."

"There are a few things I want to know too," Whitney retorted.

"Such as?"

Whitney stopped pacing and she took a couple of deep calming breaths. The red blotches faded. When she spoke, her voice was soft and faltering. "What did the clue say? The one you found at Shortcake's?" Tears stood in her eyes.

"It's not my place to tell you that."

"What type of flower was inside?"

When Kaylee hesitated, Whitney shook her head in

exasperation. "Can't you at least tell me that?"

What harm could it do? Probably none at all.

That is, if Jake had died of natural causes. But he'd been murdered. Who knew what was important and what wasn't? Who should be told what and who should be kept in the dark?

"I'm sorry, Whitney. I can't."

"You haven't figured it out, have you?"

"If you mean the clue, no. But I've learned other things."

"What do you *think* you've learned?" She was once again in-charge Whitney, with the poise and sophistication of a queen bee used to having her wishes fulfilled.

"You loved Jake. Maybe he loved you too, before he married Gina."

"That's nothing more than small-town gossip." Whitney folded her arms. "Imagine *me* with a nobody like him."

"I don't think your romance was just a rumor."

Whitney shifted her gaze to the street then down to her feet. After a moment, she raised her gaze to Kaylee.

"You're right," Whitney said. "It was a summer fling that caused me a lot of trouble and embarrassment after that boy was found dead. The sheriff made a special trip to question me, as if I had something to do with it. My parents were mortified. I don't think they ever got over it. I haven't even told them I'm here doing this promotional campaign."

"Why did you come back?"

"The opportunity came up. And since I'm still proving myself, I couldn't say no."

"What do you mean, 'proving yourself'?"

Whitney's shoulders slumped as her anger seemed to dissipate. Her expression was sad, even vulnerable.

Just as Kaylee was beginning to think Whitney would ignore the question, the young woman met her gaze. "I'm the daughter of two highly successful and highly driven parents. I want to be successful too, but not like that. Not in a profession that steals every second of my life and sucks out my soul."

She dropped her gaze to the porch railing and rubbed at a knot in the wood. "My parents, all their friends—they don't respect what I do. To them my job, my creativity, it's just me playing. They're all waiting for me to decide to grow up and do something 'real' with my life. But this?" She waved her hand, gesturing toward the street and the retail stores she'd recently filmed. "This *is* my life. I love what I do."

She met Kaylee's gaze again and gave a sad smile. "So I don't say no to opportunities. Not even when it means packing my bags and returning to Turtle Cove."

"I'm sorry," Kaylee said.

"For what?"

"Thinking you wrote the note. And also because your parents don't understand how talented you are. How you bring people together and direct your film crew and how you have to stay so organized yourself so you can keep everything else in line."

"That's high praise indeed. Thank you." Whitney picked up her bag and started for the stairs.

Kaylee stepped forward. "Jessica's husband is out of town so we're getting together for supper tonight. Would you like to join us?"

"Thanks, but I already have plans. Maybe another time."

When Whitney reached the sidewalk, Kaylee hurried to the railing and started to call after her. But she stopped herself as Whitney crossed the street and headed toward her rental car.

"It was a gardenia," Kaylee said softly, compelled to say the words she had almost shouted to Whitney. Words that needed to stay private as long as Jake's intended recipient remained an unsolved mystery.

Was the note hidden in his office desk meant for his wife? Or for the girl of his summertime dreams?

Perhaps they'd never know the answer.

17

As Kaylee carried several bags to a customer's car, Reese parked near the bakery. He hurried over to see if she needed any help.

"You're a few seconds too late," she said as she waved goodbye to her customer. "But thanks anyway."

"How about if I make it up to you with a cup of coffee?" Reese offered.

"I guess I can take a short break."

She texted Mary to let her know she was next door at the bakery while Reese ordered coffee and a small plate of holiday cookies.

"I can never resist these," Kaylee said when he placed the tray on their table. You mind if I take this?" She pointed to a pale, thick rectangle with raised lines to make it look like a snow-covered cottage. It was the only one of its kind on the plate.

"Figured you would."

"Jessica only bakes them at Christmas. I have to eat my fill of them during the holidays."

The aromatic anise-flavored cookies had been one of Kaylee's favorites since she was a child, and Jessica used a variation of Kaylee's grandmother's recipe for her bakery. Grandma had also given Jessica the special rolling pin with its indented designs that created the raised images in the rolled-out dough.

"Don't you know how to make them?" Reese asked.

"Mine never turn out right. Jessica has the touch needed to shape the dough. Besides, if I can only have them at Christmas, then they're always a special treat."

"That makes sense." He selected a ginger cookie shaped like a cartoon whale with a candy eye and icing smile. "She only makes these at Christmas too."

"It's nice to have traditions. Even little ones like cookies."

"Can't argue with that. Though other people's traditions sure are keeping me busy."

"Is that why I haven't seen you around much lately?"

"I could say the same about you. I've popped in to The Flower Patch a couple times this week, but you were always out." A mischievous grin spread across his face as he pulled out his phone. "I've decided to let you in on the secret."

"What secret?"

He tapped buttons on his phone and the grin broadened. "Jessica's daughter, Mila, took the video and sent it to me. No one else knows it even exists."

"Could you be any more mysterious?"

"Just hold on." He stifled a laugh. "Here's why the tree-lighting ceremony was discontinued. We were decorating the tree, like always, out by the lighthouse. Why Penelope thought . . . you just have to watch it."

He held the screen so they both could see it and hit play.

Kaylee covered her mouth as a crazy scene unfolded before her eyes. As Sylvia arranged garland on a tall fir, a cat leaped into the branches. A dog barked and jumped after the cat, followed closely by Sylvia's sister, Penelope, who was shouting and waving her arms.

"Is that Peaches?" Kaylee asked.

Reese, doubled over in laughter, only nodded. Kaylee took the phone from him to stop its shaking, and he held his sides. "It never gets old," he managed to say.

On the video, Sylvia made a grab for Peaches and missed. The dog, a black-and-tan collie mix, bumped into Sylvia, who struggled to maintain her balance. Penelope, in a move defying her age and Southern gentility, tackled the dog. In a tangle of garland and lights, Sylvia fell on top of Penelope. The tree swayed, smacked against the lighthouse, then ricocheted and toppled on the sisters and the dog.

"Are they hurt?" Kaylee gasped.

"Just watch."

Reese himself appeared on the screen as he, DeeDee, and Jessica tried to roll the huge tree away. Mary knelt beside it near Sylvia's and Penelope's branch-covered bodies. Peaches appeared again, bounced onto the tip of the tree then raced away, trailing a torn string of garland. The dog yelped as it crawled from beneath the pile, then took off in the opposite direction.

Once the tree was moved, Sylvia and Penelope slowly sat up in a tangle of pine needles, garland, and strands of lights.

"Mila and I call it the Christmas Cat-astrophe." Reese wiped away the tears running down his face. "And no one was physically hurt. Anyway, Sylvia swore us all to secrecy on the pain of having our deepest, darkest secrets exposed and immediately made the executive decision to move the festivities to the Sculpture Park."

"*Does* Sylvia know your deepest, darkest secrets?"

"I didn't even know I had any. But who's going to take a chance with Sylvia? Not me." He took the phone. "Let's watch it again."

After another viewing that had Kaylee laughing as much at Reese's uncontrollable laughter as the events occurring in the video, he pocketed the phone.

"You can never let Sylvia know I told you about this," he said.

"I promise. Not even to learn your deep, dark secrets," Kaylee teased. "At least that's one mystery solved."

"That reminds me. Are you still following clues with Gina?"

"We're stuck on the most recent one."

"Can I help?"

Kaylee took a moment to mentally rehearse the words, then recited, "'Petals here and petals there. A stolen kiss upon the stair. Daisies scattered everywhere.'"

"Not the best poem I've ever heard."

"It's an improvement over his others. But what does it mean?"

"Gina doesn't know? I mean, didn't Jake ever steal a kiss in their courting days?"

Kaylee merely shrugged, and Reese shook his head. "I don't think I'm going to be any help. Where did you find the other clues?"

Kaylee told him about their previous searches, but omitted her suspicion that the trail wasn't meant for Gina. She considered telling him about the anonymous note but decided against it. If neither Chad nor Whitney were responsible, then she had another mystery to solve. Reese would only worry.

"By the way," she said, suddenly remembering. "The bottom step on the back porch is loose. When you get a chance, could you take a look?"

"I can do that right now."

"You don't have to go out of your way or anything. It's minor really. More an annoyance than anything else."

"A loose step is a safety hazard. Please tell me you aren't still going in and out that way."

Kaylee showed him a face of wide-eyed innocence. "I'm not still going in and out that way."

He raised an eyebrow, clearly not believing her, then glanced at his watch. "C'mon. I've got a few minutes before my next job. If it only needs a couple of nails, I can fix it right now."

Reese stopped at his truck to get his toolbox, then headed around to the back of the mansion. Kaylee went in through the front to check with Mary and grab her coat. She hadn't worn it when helping her customer earlier, thinking she'd be quickly in and out of the cold weather.

"Hey, Bear. You want to go outside for a bit?" The dachshund wagged his tail, eager for a trip outdoors, then stood quietly while Kaylee fastened the straps on his coat. When she finished, he pranced around her feet as if showing off the latest in doggy fashion.

When Kaylee opened the back door, Bear raced down the steps toward Reese, who knelt near the bottom.

"Hey there, Bear," he said, gathering the excited dog in his arms. "You're looking fancy in that jacket."

Bear responded with a couple of barks then squirmed to get down. Soon his nose was following an invisible trail.

Reese resumed examining the step. "The board is cracked in a couple places. It needs replacing."

"Can you do that?"

"If you don't mind waiting a few days." He gave her a sharp glance. "And I meant what I said. Use the front door until I get this repaired."

"What if I'm extra careful?"

"Not even then." Reese took a measuring tape from his toolbox and handed the end to Kaylee. "Now give me a hand here."

He wrote down the dimensions of the board, then examined the other steps. "This one should probably be replaced too," he said, pointing at the adjacent board. "The others seem okay."

"Should I just have the entire thing rebuilt?"

"Up to you. Much as I hate to turn down a project, I couldn't get around to that for a while. But I can replace these two boards as a temporary measure, then rebuild the entire thing when the weather gets better."

"Whatever you think is best," Kaylee said. She sat on the top step and watched Bear play along the fence separating her lot from the bakery. Reese studied the solid wood banisters and railings, then sat beside Kaylee and scratched at the weathered paint on the banister next to him.

"I'll need to rebuild these too," he said.

"Like all home improvement projects," Kaylee said with an exaggerated sigh. "You start out with one thing and it leads to another and another and another."

Reese picked up the garden gnome that stood sentinel on the bottom step and rotated it in his hands, moving it first one way and then another as he spoke. "You know, I've been thinking about those clues. How Jake had carved an image into the brick and into the tree. You wouldn't happen to have photos, would you?"

Kaylee gave him a questioning look. "No, I never thought to take any."

"It doesn't matter." Reese put the gnome back in its spot, stood up and held out his hand. "I still may be right."

Kaylee took his hand, and he pulled her to her feet. "Right about what?"

"I've seen something like that before. Over here." He led the way to where the fence joined the corner of the mansion and bent down. "I told your grandmother about it, but she said to let it be. I think it amused her."

"What is it?"

"See for yourself." He scooted over to give Kaylee room to kneel beside him. "Right there."

A crude flower with rounded petals encircled by a heart had been carved into the fence post about a foot from the ground.

Kaylee's jaw dropped open. "I can't believe I've never noticed this before," she said.

"Why would you?"

Reese was right. She wouldn't have. A landscaping company did the routine maintenance. She and Mary occasionally talked about a redesign for this area, but so far that was all it had been, just talk. Her grandmother, with the help of the other

Petal Pushers, had already put a lovely garden in place—an impressive one, especially in the summer months—that required minimal upkeep. There really wasn't a need to change what they'd worked so hard to achieve.

"When did you say you found this?" Kaylee asked.

"Must have been shortly before Bea went to Arizona. I was taking care of a few things before the real-estate inspection."

"I wonder how long it had been here before then."

"No way to know. Does it matter?"

"Maybe." Bear pushed his nose against Kaylee's hand, and she picked him up. His feet were cold so she cradled him within her jacket. He burrowed between her arm and her chest, pushing his long nose as far beneath her elbow as he could. She barely noticed.

"What's going on in that brain of yours?" Reese asked.

"Gina thinks Jake created the trail as an anniversary surprise. But I'm not sure she's right."

"Because this isn't a recent carving," he said. "It does seem odd."

She might as well tell him. "I've been wondering if he created the trail for someone else."

"Who?"

"Whitney Mills. She's very interested in the trail—too interested. And then there are the flowers."

"What about them?"

"The first was lavender rose petals with a lavender plant. The rose petals mean 'love at first sight,' while the lavender plant means 'caution.' The strawberry blossom means 'perfect goodness,' and a gardenia symbolizes 'secret love.' Jake was a couple of years older than Gina, but they grew up together and attended the same high school for a while. How could that be love at first sight?"

Reese furrowed his brow as he thought about that. "I remember when Whitney and her family were here. I did some work for Mr. Mills. They argued about Jake—Whitney and her dad, I mean."

"They did?"

"I didn't mean to be eavesdropping, and I didn't really hear much. But her dad talked to me about it later. Asked me questions about Jake. About his family. What kind of person he was. That kind of thing."

"What did you tell him?"

"Not much. I didn't really know Jake all that well, especially not back then. If I remember right, he'd been off-island for college. Though he didn't go back after that summer. Stayed around here and bought Abner Murphy's boat-building and repair business plus the small marina from his widow."

"I wonder where he got the money to do that."

"No idea. But I have a feeling if we dig up this corner we'll find his cache. I'll get a spade." He headed for his truck, but Kaylee stopped him.

"Do you have time for this?"

"It won't take that long."

"There's a spade in the shed. I'll get the key." She placed Bear on the ground and retrieved the key from where it hung inside the mansion's back door.

After Reese found the spade, he made a rough circle in the hard ground while Kaylee stood nearby. He lifted the topsoil then dug a little deeper. A dim metallic noise sounded.

Reese met her gaze. "Found something."

After a bit more digging, Kaylee could see the outline of a metal box about the size of a cigar box. Reese pulled it out and wiped off most of the dirt.

"I can't believe it," Kaylee said. "The clue led here, to The Flower Patch. And none of us figured it out."

"Are you going to open it?"

"I don't think I should. It doesn't belong to me."

"What about finders keepers?"

"That doesn't apply here, and you know it."

"Touché," he grinned. "What are you going to do with it?"

Kaylee frowned. "We don't know if Jake created the trail for Gina or for Whitney or someone else. But we know he didn't give the first note to Whitney."

"So if he created the trail for her, he changed his mind."

"But he didn't throw away the note or destroy the caches. Wouldn't he have done that?"

"I think the answer to that died with Jake."

"Which means anything that belonged to him now belongs to Gina."

"Technically, I guess that's true."

"I don't want to cause her any more pain, and whatever is in here will probably do that, but there's no way I can give this box to Whitney." Kaylee stared at the box, then shook it gently. "No rattling," she said. "It probably has the same thing in it as the other caches. A note and a pressed flower."

"Which means another clue to follow." Reese pushed the mounded dirt back into the hole. "Give me a minute and I'll go to Gina's with you."

"Who said I was going to Gina's?"

Instead of answering, Reese gave her a look, one that said he understood her better than she understood herself. At least in moments like this when she wanted to do the right thing but couldn't be sure what that was. The answer to her dilemma could be inside the box she was holding in her hands.

But only one person had the right to open the clasps. And that person wasn't Kaylee Bleu.

"You go do whatever you need to do. I'll be fine by myself.

I can take this to Gina on my own. Just pray she doesn't have a nervous breakdown."

"Are you sure you don't want me to tag along?"

"Positive. You go to your job, and I'll take this to Gina."

She hoped she wouldn't regret not taking Reese up on his offer to go with her.

18

As Kaylee rang the doorbell, Chad pulled his beat-up truck into the driveway. Gina had probably contacted him right after Kaylee called about finding the clue at The Flower Patch. Though Kaylee was annoyed by his arrival, she couldn't blame Gina. Chad was the young widow's only family. Naturally she'd want him nearby.

"I heard you solved the clue." Chad bounded onto the stoop beside her.

Just then Gina opened the door for them. "I'm glad you're both here," she said cheerfully. "Come in out of the cold. I have the kettle on for tea. Unless you'd prefer coffee."

"Tea is fine," Kaylee said.

"For me too." Chad pecked Gina on the cheek. "Kaylee, let me take your coat."

Gina glanced at the cleaned metal box in Kaylee's hands, and her expression momentarily clouded. But she recovered quickly and beamed a smile at both of them.

"Let's sit in the kitchen," she suggested. "I've got muffins in the oven."

They followed her into the toasty room, and Kaylee set the box on the table. "Is there anything I can do to help?"

"I think you've helped enough," Chad muttered as he took a seat.

"Leave her alone, Chad. Kaylee is a good friend." Gina bustled between the table and the stove. "I appreciate everything she's done to help me."

"Thank you, Gina," Kaylee said. What else was there to say?

Chad might be upset that she'd told Gina instead of him about finding the clue, but she'd never promised she would.

Once the tea and muffins were ready, Gina joined them at the table. She stared at the box, but didn't touch it.

"What do you think is inside?" she asked.

"I'm sure Kaylee can tell us," Chad said.

"We didn't open it," Kaylee protested.

"We?"

"Reese Holt was with me. Actually, he's the one who solved the clue. Except he didn't actually solve it. He just knew about the carved flower."

"What carved flower?" Chad pressed.

"Reese had seen it before. When I told him about the other carvings, he remembered this one. It was on a fence post at the corner of the mansion. Reese had seen it once when—" she stopped abruptly. They didn't need to know how long ago Reese had seen the flower.

"When what?"

"Stop giving her the third degree," Gina said. "You're being rude."

"I'm only trying to understand how Reese got involved in your business," Chad insisted.

"Reese had done some work back there," Kaylee intervened. "He saw the carving then, but it didn't mean anything to him."

"Convenient that it suddenly did." Chad broke his muffin in two, scattering crumbs on the table.

"All that matters," Gina said, "is that Kaylee and Reese found the box. I just hope this is the end of the trail."

The only way to know was to open the box, but no one pointed that out. Instead a silence seemed to descend upon them. After a few moments, Chad squeezed Gina's hand.

"Do you remember when we were kids? We used to talk about

leaving the island someday. We were going to be stowaways."

"I remember."

"We can do that now, Gina. I don't mean stow away. But we can go anywhere we want. Start over."

Gina stared at him as if he had sprouted horns. "Why would we start over?"

He glanced at Kaylee, and suddenly she felt like an intruder in an intimate family drama.

"I should probably be leaving—"

"Please don't," Gina pleaded. "I'd like you to be here. You're part of this too."

Kaylee responded with a polite smile. *It seems that way. Whether I want to be or not.*

"Gina, I'm serious." Chad regained his sister's attention. "You've got money now. Or you will have once the insurance check comes through and you sell the business. We don't have to stay here."

"We're not kids anymore, Chad. We're islanders. We'll always be islanders." She placed her hands in her lap. "You can start over somewhere else if you want to. But I'm staying."

Chad flopped back in his chair without even trying to hide his exasperation. He flipped a hand at the box. "Open it then." He glared at Kaylee. "I just hope it's the last one."

"So do I," Kaylee said. Then she could concentrate on her work instead of someone else's puzzles.

Gina looked from one to the other, then stared at the box. Her shoulders appeared rigid, and for a moment Kaylee wondered if she was going to faint. Perhaps she also suspected the box wasn't meant for her. Would the contents confirm that? Kaylee wished she was anywhere but sitting in this delightful kitchen with these strange siblings.

Suddenly, in one quick motion, Gina snapped open the

clasps and flipped up the lid. "It's another pressed flower," she said, turning the box toward Kaylee.

Kaylee picked up the delicate pink blossoms clustered at the end of a stem. "Most likely a cherry blossom. *Prunus serrulata.* At least that's the most popular variety. Vancouver has a cherry blossom festival every April. They're beautiful that time of year. It's a popular tourist attraction."

"I'll have to put it on my bucket list," Chad said wryly.

Kaylee ignored him as she tried to decipher Jake's floriographic message.

Love at first sight. Caution. Perfect goodness. Secret love.

And now a cherry blossom. *Transience of life.*

Ironic considering Jake was now dead.

"Is there a note?" Gina asked.

Kaylee moved the tissue paper and pulled out another sheet of the blue stationery. She held it out to Gina, but she shook her head. "You read it."

Kaylee exchanged an uncomfortable glance with Chad, who nodded curtly. She bit her lip and unfolded the note.

Storey builds

Stone upon stone

The view we see

Is ours alone.

Tears filled Gina's eyes and slipped along her cheeks. "Why did he do this to me? I wish I'd never found that first note." She abruptly stood and ran from the room.

When Chad didn't move, Kaylee pushed back her chair.

"Let her be," he said, his voice soft and surprisingly kind considering his words. "An audience only makes it worse."

"That seems like a cruel thing to say."

"I don't mean it that way. It's just part of who Gina is. She can't get control of herself unless she's alone."

"I'll go then," Kaylee carried her dishes to the counter by the sink. "I'm truly sorry this wasn't the end."

"She'll be okay, given some time." Chad rubbed his jaw. "At least Jake isn't around anymore. That's all that really matters."

"Excuse me?" Kaylee asked warily.

"'Don't speak ill of the dead.' That's what everybody says. But now I don't have to stay up nights worrying about Gina. About what he might do to her."

"What are you saying?"

"My brother-in-law was the one who punched me. I never told anybody because I knew how it would look. That maybe he had a heart attack because we were fighting. Then it turns out he was murdered. I definitely didn't have anything to do with that."

"Are you a suspect?"

"Sheriff Maddox questioned me. Luckily I have an alibi."

Kaylee didn't want to ask her next question. But she had to know. "Did Jake hurt Gina?"

"He hadn't yet. But I figured it was just a matter of time."

"Why do you think that?"

He sighed heavily. "Gina had a boyfriend. Derek Glasser."

"I've heard of him."

"Then you know he died that summer. When Whitney Mills was here with her family."

Fear gripped Kaylee's stomach as her mind raced ahead, jumping to one crazy conclusion after another. Her throat, suddenly paralyzed, prevented her from speaking. But Chad didn't need any encouragement.

"They said it was an accident. But I never believed it."

Kaylee sipped the last of her tea. She wanted out of this house, which had lost its cozy charm, but she also wanted to hear what Chad had to say. "What do you think happened?" she finally managed to ask.

Chad's head was bent over the table as if a heavy weight pressed against him. "Derek was practically engaged to my sister," he said. "Then he lost his head over Whitney, but she was Jake's girl."

He raised his eyes to Kaylee's and his solemn expression turned her blood to ice.

"So Jake killed him."

19

"Do you really believe that?" Kaylee asked.

"I don't have any proof," Chad said. "But I never trusted Jake after Derek died. I didn't want Gina to marry him." He shook his head. "After that summer Gina and Jake were inseparable. She got over Derek, and he got over Whitney. At least I thought he did."

"But not now?"

"It's always been a mystery how Jake had enough money to take over Abner Murphy's business. Gina believed all that bunk that he'd saved it." Chad snorted in disbelief. "That's why we fought. He got drunk, and I was trying to sober him up. And he told me, flat-out told me Whitney's dad had paid him to leave her alone. He took the money, but he meant to have Whitney too. He never cared about Gina."

"He must have had some feelings for her," Kaylee said. "Or he wouldn't have married her."

"He married her on the rebound because Whitney took off." Chad leaned forward, elbows pressed against the table, and stared up at Kaylee. "What if Jake knew Whitney was coming back? Maybe he hid all these clues to impress her."

Chad might have been right except for one thing: The trail wasn't recent.

But that didn't mean Jake hadn't known Whitney was returning to the island. Kaylee tried to remember what Whitney had said about being a last-minute replacement for the original promotional company. But she couldn't remember if that had been before or after Jake's death.

Her mind was whirling with speculation. And trying to find

a gracious way to get out of this house.

Just leave.

"I've got to go," she said. "I've already stayed longer than I intended."

"I'll get your coat," Chad said flatly.

As she passed by the table, Kaylee picked up the latest clue and read it to herself. "He misspelled *story*. But the rhythm isn't bad."

"What did you say?"

"The rhythm isn't bad."

"No. About *story*." Chad took the note, scanned the page, then an eager smile brightened his expression. "We might as well see this through. I know where to find the next clue."

Kaylee pulled into the parking lot at the top of Mount Constitution the following morning next to Chad's pickup and stared out her windshield at the spectacular view.

The mountain had the distinction of being the highest point on Orcas Island and the other San Juan Islands. A stone observation tower, built in the 1930s and patterned to resemble a medieval watchtower, loomed skyward and allowed visitors to climb even higher. On a clear day, it was sometimes possible to see all the way to Vancouver, or even to Victoria in British Columbia.

She climbed out of her SUV and wondered for the hundredth time whether she should have brought Jessica or DeeDee with her. Not that she was afraid of Chad, but the mountain was isolated this time of year. Who knew what they might find here, or how Gina would react?

Speaking of Gina, where was she?

"I almost gave up on you," Chad said, coming up behind her.

Kaylee jumped then pressed her hand against her chest while she caught her breath.

"Sorry," he said. "Didn't mean to scare you."

"It's okay." It was all she could do to keep the annoyance out of her voice. "Where's Gina?"

"She wouldn't come. Said she was tired of Jake's games." He seemed sad. "I think she knows."

"Knows what?"

"The trail wasn't meant for her."

"Then why are we here?"

"She asked me to follow it to the end. I intend to do that."

But why am I *here?*

There seemed no easy answer to that question. For her own inexplicable reasons, Gina wanted Kaylee involved in Jake's treasure hunt even if she'd given up on it. Kaylee doubted even Gina could put her reasons into words. The girl was an emotional mess, and Kaylee didn't think it was just because of her husband's unsolved murder. She needed therapy to resolve issues going back to her tumultuous childhood.

And so did Chad. He might hide his emotional wounds better than his sister, but they were within him.

"Why do you stay?" Kaylee asked, surprising herself as much as Chad with the question.

"What?"

"Just because Gina doesn't want to leave the island doesn't mean you can't. Believe me, I know it's a big step to move away from your home. But if it's something you really want to do, you should do it."

"Who would look after Gina?"

"She has friends. There are people on this island who care about her. Besides, maybe Gina needs to take care of herself."

"She's not capable of that."

"How do you know?" Kaylee dug the toe of her boot into the gravel. She was treading on dangerous ground here. But something needed to be said, and maybe she was the only one who could say it. "Has she ever had the chance to try?"

The sound of an engine caught Kaylee's attention. A car came into view, and Kaylee gasped in disbelief.

Whitney parked and climbed out of the car.

Chad didn't bother to disguise the disgust he was obviously feeling. "What are you doing here?" he demanded as she approached them.

"I thought I could help. Whatever you find belongs to me. You have to know that." When neither Kaylee nor Chad responded, Whitney's eyes narrowed. "You didn't already find it, did you?"

"I just got here," Kaylee said. "As you know since you were behind me."

Whitney glared at Chad.

"I looked around, but no." He shrugged his shoulders. "It's a big place."

"Tell me the clue. I'll help you find it."

Kaylee and Chad exchanged glances.

"She might as well since she's already here," Kaylee said. Besides, the sooner they found the cache, the better. Then they could all go home, and she could get back to work. She had a feeling this was the last one. The spectacular setting invoked the feeling of a dramatic finish.

Chad frowned and then recited Jake's latest rhyme.

"It's *storey* with an e," Kaylee explained when Chad finished. "S-t-o-r-e-y."

Whitney's mouth curved up in a small, sad smile. "Ellsworth Storey." She gazed at the stone tower. "The architect."

"He designed this," Chad said.

"I know. Jake told me all about it when we hiked up here. He was a big fan of old Ellsworth." She sauntered to a nearby picnic table and perched on it. "Good luck."

"I thought you were going to help," Kaylee said.

"No need." Whitney sat on the table. "I'm pretty sure I know where he hid the clue."

"Then why don't you get it?" Chad said.

"My clue. My secret."

Kaylee joined Whitney at the picnic table.

"It's cold up here, and I want to go back to town," Kaylee said.

"Go ahead." Whitney shoved her hands into her coat pockets. "I'm not stopping you."

"I'm not leaving as long as she's still here," Chad said as he joined them. "Whatever Jake left behind belongs to Gina."

"It belongs to me."

"Prove it," Chad demanded.

"I know what Gina doesn't. The significance of each location and the meaning of each flower." Whitney crossed her arms and hunched her shoulders against the brisk mountaintop wind. "I did a research project on the language of flowers for a Brit Lit class in college. The topic fascinated me—still does in fact. Jake knew that."

"Then why didn't you know where to look at Shortcake Bistro?" Kaylee asked. "You were searching the gallery."

"You found it in a tree, didn't you?" Whitney smirked, taking Kaylee's surprise as confirmation. "I figured that's where Jake had hidden the clue, but I could hardly climb the tree while you were still there. I thought if I seemed absorbed in the gallery that would throw you off the scent. Unfortunately, you found the clue before I made it back there."

Whitney's face took on a wistful expression. "I love strawberries. Plain ones, chocolate-dipped ones, strawberry shortcake, strawberry ice cream. And because Jake loved me, he loved strawberries too."

Kaylee remembered her conversation with Gina about the clue that led to the historic barreling plant. Gina had said that Jake hated strawberries, that he never ate them. Perhaps because they reminded him of Whitney, his love at first sight, his secret love? Were the memories too painful for him?

Although, the memories hadn't kept him from marrying Gina after Whitney left.

Gina must have known she was his rebound. Or perhaps she'd been too in love with him to care. Or maybe it was as simple as two people consoling each other in their grief. Gina mourning Derek's death, and Jake heartbroken because Whitney had abandoned him.

"Why didn't you stay on the island with Jake?" Kaylee asked gently.

A cloud darkened Whitney's expression, but she merely shook her head. "It no longer matters."

"I bet I know why." Chad stepped close, his body language intimidating as he hovered over the women. "She left because she killed Derek."

"I did not!"

Kaylee stared at Chad in surprise. "You told me yesterday you thought Jake killed Derek."

"I did. Until she showed up here today. Think about it, Kaylee. It makes sense. She killed Derek, and now she's killed Jake."

Whitney jumped to her feet. "I did no such thing. How can you say that?"

"Because it's true." Chad's chin jutted out, emphasizing his words as he stared at Whitney. "Did Jake know you killed Derek? Is that why you had to shut him up? It can't be a coincidence you came to the island so soon after he died."

"Chad," Kaylee said, trying to placate him and Whitney both. Of all the situations she'd gotten herself into over the past couple of years, this had to be one of the craziest: standing on top of Mount Constitution with two angry people and apparently two unsolved murders. The accusations and denials swirled around her until she'd had enough.

"Stop it, both of you," she said in her most severe professorial voice. "Here's the plan. Chad, you stop making wild accusations you can't back up. Whitney, if you know where Jake's cache is hidden, get it now."

"You can't make me," Whitney said.

"What are you, in middle school?" Kaylee retorted. "Go."

Whitney threw up her hands. "All right. I think it'll be on the other side of the tower. It was where Jake kissed me for the first time."

"How romantic." Chad's words dripped with sarcasm.

"This way," Whitney said, ignoring him. They followed her to the other side of the tower near the overlook sign. "It's probably around here somewhere."

Chad scanned the surrounding area then pointed to a small pile of rocks near the base of a larger boulder. "Looks like someone stacked those on purpose."

"A double meaning," Kaylee said. "The clue says, 'stone upon stone.'"

"Very good." Chad appeared almost impressed then he climbed over the railing and carefully slid down a short incline. As he began to move the rocks, Kaylee joined him.

"I can do this myself," Chad said.

"I know," Kaylee said simply. She also knew Chad could easily deny finding a clue if no one else was close by. Whitney must have had a similar thought because she also joined them.

Chad frowned, which only confirmed Kaylee's theory about

his intentions. He moved a few more rocks, and Kaylee spied the edge of the now-familiar oilcloth. She quickly bent down and tugged the package from beneath the remaining rocks.

"I'll open it." Chad reached for the package, but Kaylee stuck it behind her back.

"That's not happening," she said.

"Now who's the middle schooler?" Chad asked.

Kaylee ignored the comment. "I'll call Sheriff Maddox and ask him to meet us at my house. Chad, you call Gina and tell her to come too. When we're all there you can tell the sheriff about your suspicions." She turned to Whitney. "And you can tell him anything else you've kept secret about that summer."

"All the clues, all the flowers belong to me," Whitney said.

"We'll see. For all I know these clues are evidence in an unsolved murder. I'm the only forensics expert here."

"Only in flowers," Chad said.

"Still counts." Kaylee headed back up the incline. "Now let's go."

20

Kaylee sat at the head of her dining room table with Sheriff Maddox and Whitney on one side, Gina and Chad on the other. Jessica and Mary occupied the seats at the other end of the table. The package, still wrapped in the oilcloth, was on a place mat in front of Kaylee.

Mary and Jessica had arrived at Wildflower Cottage first, letting themselves in with Kaylee's hidden key, and prepared sandwiches, salads, coffee, and tea. Kaylee was reminded again how lucky she was to have such wonderful friends. The food seemed to take the edge from everyone's bristled feelings.

"I guess the first thing to do is open it," Sheriff Maddox said in his straightforward manner.

Kaylee unwrapped the package. It contained another Le Soleil commemorative tin.

"You and Jake ate a lot of candy that summer," Chad said.

Whitney shot him a dirty look, but didn't say anything.

Kaylee took the lid off the tin and lifted out a pressed flower with purple petals.

"It's a *Cleome hassleriana*. A spider flower."

Kaylee and Whitney glanced at each other, and all the blood seemed to rush from Whitney's face.

"What's wrong?" Sheriff Maddox said.

"In the language of flowers," Kaylee explained reluctantly, "a spider flower means 'elope with me.'"

Gina gasped, and Kaylee's heart ached for the young widow. But it ached for Whitney too.

"What else is in the box?" the sheriff asked.

Kaylee removed the tissue paper and pulled out a blue envelope that matched the stationery the other notes had been written on. "It's addressed *To My Only Love*."

She shifted her gaze from Whitney, who seemed about to pass out at any moment, to Gina, who didn't look much better.

"Read it, Kaylee," Sheriff Maddox said. "It's best to get all this out in the open."

Kaylee carefully opened the flap and slid out the note. One glance told her all she needed to know.

She showed the note to the sheriff without reading it completely.

He skimmed it, then asked, "Mrs. Beckett, when did you and your husband start dating?"

Gina answered automatically, without emotion. "We started seeing each other after Derek died. Just as friends at first. Then we realized we were in love. We got married before Christmas."

"This note was written before Derek's death." Sheriff Maddox slid it back into the envelope and placed it in the box. "But since there's no name on the letter, I only have your word, Ms. Mills, that the note is intended for you."

"As I told Kaylee and Chad before, I can tell you the story behind each location and each flower," Whitney said quietly. "And I knew where to find this box."

"Can you solve the clue Kaylee found at Shortcake's?" Gina asked, her face stony.

"Probably."

Gina pulled the note from her bag and handed it to Whitney. As she read the clue, a sad smile appeared.

"The next clue was hidden near the fence post between The Flower Patch and the bakery."

"How did you know?" Kaylee asked.

"It was our secret meeting place. One of them anyway. I'd buy a flower or a lavender soap and then slip out the back door.

Jake would come from the rear of the bakery. No one ever saw us." She turned to Kaylee. "What was the flower?"

"A cherry blossom. It means *transience of life,*" Kaylee explained to the others.

"Seems an odd message to give your girlfriend," the sheriff said.

"Not really," Whitney said. "Jake was reminding me that life is short. We needed to grab our dreams when we could. It's something he'd say when we talked about the future."

"Let's not get all misty-eyed here," Chad said. "Maybe it's true Jake left the flowers and the notes for Whitney. But no one is saying anything about who murdered Jake. Or Derek for that matter. I'm putting my money on her." He pointed to Whitney.

"No need for dramatics," the sheriff said. "And what makes you think the Glasser boy was murdered?"

"Well, it's fishy, isn't it? Derek dies and Whitney suddenly breaks it off with her—" he made air quotes "'—secret love.'"

"I told you before, I didn't hurt Derek. I wouldn't." Whitney grabbed her bag and dug through it. "The only thing I'm guilty of is taking these." She placed Jake's first note and one of the commemorative tins on the table.

"You broke into my house?" Gina said. "You're the criminal mastermind?"

"I'm sorry, Gina," Whitney said. "I truly am. But I had to see the clues, to see what Jake had left. I thought it might give me some kind of closure about his death."

"What about the anonymous note to Kaylee?" Mary asked. "Did you put it on her windshield?"

Guilt tightened Whitney's expression. "I knew if I could get the clue you found at the strawberry plant that I could follow the rest of the trail myself. But I had to stop you from getting to the other clues first."

She shifted in her chair to face the sheriff. "I know it was wrong, and I'm sorry. But please don't arrest me. Or make me wear handcuffs. I'll go with you if I have to."

Gina abruptly stood from the table. "There's no need to arrest her. She can have all the clues. I won't be pressing any charges."

"But you can't just let her go, Sheriff." Chad stood too, and put his arm around his sister. "Don't you see? She killed Derek. Or she knew Jake did—or she helped him—and kept quiet about it all these years. That makes her an accessory. Then she came back here and killed Jake."

"No she didn't," Gina's voice caught, and tears glistened in her dark eyes. "I know what happened to Jake."

Chad froze, then whispered, "How can you?"

The sheriff rose from his seat and handed Gina his handkerchief. "Who was it, Gina?" he asked softly.

Gina shook her head.

"She doesn't know, Sheriff," Chad said. "You can see how upset she is."

Gina pushed away from her brother. "I'm okay."

"Who, Gina?" the sheriff repeated.

"Nobody killed him."

Kaylee noted the relief evident on Chad's face, but as soon as he realized she was watching him, he tensed again. Who did he think Gina was going to name?

A confession!

Was that it? Was that why Chad was so eager to blame first Jake, then Whitney for Derek's death? A death that had already been ruled an accident. Was he afraid Gina was the murderer?

Gina took another deep breath then stared at her hands. "Jake killed himself."

Kaylee stared at Gina, then at Jessica and Mary. They seemed just as shocked. Only Sheriff Maddox managed to keep his composure at Gina's pronouncement.

"Why do you say that, Gina?"

"It was the wine bottle. There was a little bit of wine left and I drank it, but it made me sick. I think there was something in it."

"Do you still have the bottle?"

"It's at the marina."

Kaylee thought back to the day she had gone to the office with Gina. She had shown Kaylee the wine bottle then. How strange to think that the "murder weapon" had been in plain sight. But how could they have known?

"Anyone could have put those antibiotics in the wine," she said. "And alibis are useless. Whoever did this didn't have to stick around. All they had to do was wait."

"I have serious doubts that Jake poisoned himself," the sheriff said to Gina. "The important thing now is to examine that bottle. I need to make a call."

Once he got Deputy Garcia on the phone, the sheriff instructed her to hightail it to the marina office and be sure no one went in or out of the building until he arrived. When he finished the call, he turned to Gina. "Let's go take a gander at that bottle, shall we?"

Kaylee drove Gina's car to the marina while the young widow sat in the passenger seat and stared out the window. She periodically dabbed at her eyes with a tissue clutched in her hand. Chad followed in his truck.

Everybody had wanted to go to the marina, but Sheriff Maddox put the kibosh on that plan. Instead he arranged for Mary and Jessica to take Whitney to his office while he led the convoy to the marina.

Once everyone was inside the office, Gina pointed to the bottle. It stood on the counter next to a glass that contained wine residue.

"Print them both," Sheriff Maddox said to Robyn, "then send them to the Seattle lab. I want a complete report on that residue."

Robyn immediately bagged both the bottle and the glass. The sheriff looked around the office, but he didn't find anything else of interest. Kaylee watched Gina and Chad, seated next to each other on the worn sofa, but they didn't have much to say. Gina had shut down, staring at nothing while Chad feigned disinterest.

When the sheriff and Robyn were ready to leave, Kaylee considered asking Gina to stay the night with her at Wildflower Cottage. But before she could make the offer, Chad spoke up.

"Come on, Gina," he said. "We'll swing by my place so I can pick up a few things. Then I'll take you home."

"You'll stay with her?" Sheriff Maddox asked. "That's good."

"It's what families do for each other," Chad said defensively. "Isn't it?"

"Sure is, son," the sheriff replied. "It sure is."

But not the Sinclair family. At least not where the parents were concerned. Otherwise, at least one of them would be with Gina during this difficult time.

Kaylee gave Chad an encouraging smile as he led Gina from the office. At least Gina had her brother by her side.

While Kaylee was outside with Bear for his last run of the night, headlights appeared in her driveway. As the vehicle drew nearer, she recognized it as Whitney's rental.

What in the world is she doing back here?

Whitney joined Kaylee on the porch. Her face was as white as a ghost, and her hands were shaking. "We need to talk," she said.

"What happened?"

"They found my prints on that bottle."

Would this mystery never be solved? "Let's go inside."

When they were settled in the den, Kaylee faced Whitney. "Tell me."

"I gave Jake that wine. I came to see him a few days before my 'official' arrival."

"You mean you were here before he died? In Turtle Cove?"

Whitney nodded. "I hadn't seen him, hadn't even talked to him since I left that summer. But I needed to explain. I got this assignment, and I didn't want to run into him for the first time in a crowd or at the bakery. I didn't want him to be surprised I was back."

"Why are you telling me this?"

"I'm not sure. I guess because you're honest."

"I try to be."

"So do I. But Sheriff Maddox is mad that I didn't say anything about the wine bottle before they ran the prints."

"Why didn't you?"

"I don't know. I suppose part of me hoped Gina was talking about a different bottle. Though I should have known better. Jake wasn't much of a drinker. I don't know why I even brought him the bottle. I guess it was supposed to be a kind of peace offering."

"I'm guessing he didn't tell Gina about your visit."

"He must not have, or she would have said something. I'm not sure the sheriff believes my story, but it's true. I didn't poison that wine."

"If the sheriff thought you had, he'd have put you in jail."

"We came to an agreement." Whitney lifted her pants leg to

reveal an ankle bracelet. "There's another condition too."

"What's that?"

"He said he'd be much obliged if you'd put me up for the night." She glanced at her watch. "He'll be calling within the next ten minutes. To be sure I didn't disappear. Not that there's anywhere to hide on this island."

Kaylee wasn't too sure about that. It would certainly be possible to find a place to lay low, at least short-term.

"You've got to believe me. I didn't kill Jake." Whitney wrung her hands and hung her head a moment before meeting Kaylee's gaze. "But I think Jake killed Derek."

"Wasn't Derek's death ruled an accident?"

"That doesn't mean it *was* an accident."

"Why do you think Jake was responsible?"

"They'd argued. Derek didn't know Jake and I were seeing each other, and he started hanging around me. I tried to discourage him, but he wouldn't take no for an answer. Finally, Jake got involved. Derek threatened to tell my parents about Jake. The next day he was dead."

"You really believe Jake killed him?"

"I was so afraid. I persuaded my parents to leave immediately." She leaned her head back, eyes closed. "It was only supposed to be a summer fling, but I did care about Jake. Part of me still does. But I could never have—"

Her voice broke as she collapsed into tears.

Kaylee's phone rang. "Hi, Sheriff."

"She there?"

"Yes."

"I owe you one."

More than one.

"Is she pouring out her heart?"

"Pretty much."

"Good. Just remember that anything she tells you is confidential. Nobody else knows about her sneak trip into town before Jake's death, not even Gina."

"How can you be sure?"

"Because Gina has no idea where the wine bottle came from. Of course her prints are on it too, but I don't think that means anything."

"Except for reasonable doubt to a good defense attorney."

"That's right. And since Ms. Mills, or at least her family, can afford the best, we need to cross all our t's before making an arrest."

"For what it's worth, I don't think she did it."

"Me neither. Oh, and just so you know, we're reopening the Derek Glasser case."

"You believe Whitney's story?"

"I can't ignore it. Especially after all that 'language of flowers' stuff. It's not common knowledge, but jasmine petals were found around the pier where Derek's skiff was found."

"A jasmine means 'eternal and unconditional love.' So Jake might have been there."

"Never took Jake for such a romantic," the sheriff said. "Still, that isn't really proof."

"Maybe whoever killed Jake believes he killed Derek, whether he did or not. It was payback."

"Are you referring to Chad?"

"I'm not referring to anyone in particular."

There was a pause before the sheriff spoke again. "Can I ask another favor? Take a look at the Glasser file for me."

"Sure. I can come by sometime tomorrow."

"No need. I gave a copy to Robyn. She'll bring it to The Flower Patch in the morning. Maybe you'll see something we missed."

They finished their conversation and Kaylee returned to the den. Whitney had curled up in the chair, still crying. Kaylee resumed her seat but didn't say anything. Perhaps the best thing was for Whitney to release all the tears she needed for her summer romance.

Kaylee suddenly realized that Jake had expressed a deep love for Whitney with his pressed flowers and clues. What was it the sheriff had said? He didn't know Jake had such a romantic side? But Whitney considered the relationship as only a summer fling. And she thought him capable of murder—but why?

Men sometimes fought over women. But that didn't mean they killed each other.

But Derek had been found dead, and Whitney had fled.

Did she know something she still wasn't telling?

21

Kaylee was ringing up a purchase when Chad came into The Flower Patch the next day. He browsed among the displays until the customer left then sauntered toward the counter.

"Hi, Chad. How's Gina this morning?"

"She's been better. I thought a bouquet of flowers might cheer her up. Ones that don't say anything about love."

"Different sources sometimes give different meanings for the same flower. Flowers mean what we want them to."

"Apparently Jake didn't think so. At least not when it came to Whitney. I never saw him give Gina flowers. Guess now we know why."

Kaylee didn't want to get into a conversation about Jake's love life. The best thing to do was give Chad what he wanted so he'd leave. Besides, she had a ton of work to do and Mary wouldn't be in until later in the day.

"What do you think of tulips? I have a few pink ones."

"What do tulips mean?"

"The pink ones mean caring."

"I'll take them." He pulled out his wallet.

"Do you want me to deliver them?"

"Nah. I'll take them to her. She needs me to look at her car again."

"What's wrong with it now?"

"One thing and then another."

"She sure seems to have a lot of trouble with it. Strange since it doesn't seem to be that old."

"Guess she got herself a lemon."

Something about his offhanded manner made the hairs on

Kaylee's neck stand up. Could Chad have been deliberately sabotaging the car, perhaps as a means of controlling his sister? She mentally swatted away the thought. She was probably just tired. Yesterday had been a long day, and she and Whitney had stayed up way too late.

Whitney had dragged herself into the kitchen that morning as Kaylee was getting ready to leave, and she'd begged Kaylee to leave Bear with her. Kaylee had reluctantly agreed, a decision she now regretted. But she knew from her own experience how comforting it was to have the happy little dog nearby.

Kaylee reached for an order form. "Do you want a vase or a boxed arrangement?"

"Whatever's faster," Chad said. "I can't be hanging around here all day."

"No vase then. How about half a dozen tied with a gold ribbon?"

Chad nodded approval, and Kaylee headed toward the workroom. Chad followed her. She didn't know what was worse, the idea of him hanging around unsupervised in the showroom or that he thought it was okay to invade her work space. Though, in retrospect, she had done the same thing to him.

"I stopped by the hotel to see Whitney this morning," Chad said, "but she wasn't there. Do you think she's left the island? Or maybe she's lounging in a jail cell."

"Why would she be in jail?" Kaylee asked.

"For killing Jake."

"There's no proof she did that."

"She gave him that bottle of wine, didn't she?"

"I'm really not comfortable talking about Whitney. Or Jake." Kaylee gathered six tulip buds from the cooler and placed them on a bed of ferns.

"I wouldn't be surprised if she ran away. That's what she did before."

Kaylee didn't respond, concentrating instead on wrapping the tulips in tissue paper and tying an elaborate bow.

"People like her the same way they like her dad. That whole family thinks they can do whatever they want, spread around a little money, and get away with anything. Like how Whitney would flirt with Derek when no one else was around, then pretend she didn't know who he was if anyone was watching."

"If no one else was around, how do you know she did that?"

"We were tight, Derek and me. Said he told her he was dating Gina, but that didn't mean anything to her. And now to find out she was stringing Jake along too. He sure had it bad for her, didn't he? Makes you wonder—"

Despite herself, Kaylee was caught up in Chad's musings. Especially since they seemed to contradict what he'd said before about Jake having no intention of breaking up his romance with Whitney despite taking what must have been a substantial amount of money from her father.

"Wonder what?" she heard herself asking.

"How often Whitney came to the island without anyone seeing her. Anyone but Jake that is."

Kaylee's blood turned cold and her fingers fumbled with the bow.

"Whitney came to the island?" She tried to make it sound like an innocent question—as if she didn't already know about Whitney's secret visit.

"Just before Jake died."

"How do you know?"

"Gina told me."

"But Gina didn't know."

Chad's expression darkened, and he toyed with an assortment of ribbons. "You say that with such certainty. But how could you know what Gina knows?"

Kaylee's mouth felt dry and she did her best to moisten her lips. How could she answer such a crazy question? Especially when the sheriff had told her not to mention Whitney's trip to see Jake.

Her thoughts sped to a startling—and frightening—conclusion.

Whitney hadn't told Chad about her trip. Gina didn't know. That could only mean one thing.

"Jake told you." She met Chad's dark gaze. "Didn't he?"

Chad tilted his head and any pretense of congeniality disappeared. "Gina was right about you. It seems you do have a talent for solving mysteries. Unmasking the murderer."

"I don't know who killed Jake." Her heart rate sped up.

"Maybe you didn't a moment ago." Chad's eyes narrowed. "But I think you know now."

"So what if Jake told you about Whitney's visit? That's not a motive for murder. That doesn't mean you killed him," she said, stalling for time.

Though deep inside Kaylee knew he had. Jake and Chad had fought but Chad hadn't really said why. Only that he was worried about Gina. There were other indications too, albeit small ones. Like how nervous Chad had been last night when Gina said she knew what happened to Jake. How relieved he'd been when she said Jake had killed himself.

"You suspect me." Chad's voice interrupted her thoughts. "Don't you?"

Kaylee briefly shut her eyes, thankful the worktable was between them, but knowing she needed to get out of there fast. At least Bear wasn't here. He was safe and couldn't be used as leverage to force her to cooperate.

"Why would you kill him, Chad?"

"Because I couldn't take the risk any longer that he'd hurt Gina. Jake killed Derek. He tried to pretend it was an accident, that they were fighting, and Derek hit his head on the pier. But if that was true, why didn't Jake own up to it instead of putting Derek in the skiff and setting him adrift?"

"Sometimes people panic and do things that don't make sense later." She focused on the ribbon twisted between her fingers and hoped Deputy Garcia would show up soon with those files.

Chad walked the length of the table, and Kaylee cautiously kept her distance on the other side.

"And then do you know what Jake did? When Whitney wouldn't talk to him, wouldn't see him, he made my sister believe he loved her."

"Perhaps he did." Where was Deputy Garcia?

"No!" Chad shouted then took a deep breath as if to calm himself. "No," he said in a hushed tone, made more sinister by its lack of volume. "I know the truth because Jake told me. He was feeling all sorry for himself because Whitney had come and gone again. Came to tell him she had a job here in Turtle Cove, but it'd be best if they stayed away from each other. Wanted him to know they were just friends. Had always been just friends."

She had to keep him talking. "It sounds like his feelings were hurt."

"Hurt enough that he no longer cared he was talking to his wife's brother. 'I still love her,' he said. 'We belong together.'" Chad sneered. "What about Gina? She adored him, and he didn't care. He never really cared about her. If he'd left her, she'd have had nothing. At least now she has the insurance money."

"She might not if his death is ruled a suicide. It depends on what's in the policy."

"We can't let that happen, can we?" Chad smirked. "Whitney's to blame. You see, I did a bit of sleuthing of my own. The lab will find traces of an antibiotic in that wine bottle—the same antibiotic mentioned in that medical report the sheriff gave Gina.

Would you like to take a guess who has a prescription for that exact same medication?"

"Whitney?"

Chad shook his head in mock sorrow. "She really shouldn't leave medication in her purse, and she should watch her purse more carefully in public. It was too easy to sneak that pill bottle when she wasn't looking. It was also easy to put the ground-up pills in a bottle of wine, meet her at the store, and then just happen to suggest that she take it to Jake as a peace offering." His expression became fierce. "She's going to pay for what happened to Derek. And for breaking my sister's heart."

"I think you're the one who did that when you killed Gina's husband."

"She'll never know that. Even if she makes the connection about the antibiotics and Whitney, she'll think Whitney killed Jake." He slipped his hand in his pocket and pulled out a revolver. "I came prepared. I'm always prepared."

Kaylee stood frozen, but willed herself to speak. "To kill me? Why? I wouldn't even know you killed Jake if you hadn't told me."

"You're too smart for your own good. You'd have figured it out, just like you did all those clues Jake left behind. I can't take that chance."

Kaylee's heart raced and her hands trembled. "So you're going to shoot me here in my own shop?"

"Don't be stupid." He waved the gun toward the rear of the house. "We're going for a drive. And somewhere along the way, on a quiet, deserted road, you're going to have car trouble and lose control. No one will ever find out what you know."

Despite her fear, Kaylee managed to put on a facade of courage. "Like you gave Gina car trouble? I won't go."

He extended his arm, pointing the revolver at her head. "I think you will."

Think, Kaylee, think. The best thing to do was cooperate, or at least pretend to, until she had an opportunity to—

She knew what to do. "I need my keys. They're in my bag."

He kept the gun aimed at her while he found the keys, then motioned for her to precede him out the rear door. As they crossed the threshold, he grabbed her arm and stuck the revolver against her ribs. When they reached the edge of the porch, Kaylee hesitated a moment and took a deep breath.

This was the best chance she was going to have.

As they descended the porch, Kaylee stepped on one side of the broken step, which forced Chad to step on the cracked part. His foot slipped as the wood splintered, and she knocked into him. Then she grabbed the gnome and smacked him in the gut. As he bent over, the gun went off. Kaylee couldn't take any more chances. She whacked him over the head. The gnome broke and the gun fell, hitting the cobblestones.

Kaylee snatched up the gun and aimed it at Chad, but she needn't have bothered. He was sprawled across the steps, completely unconscious. A trail of blood seeped down his pants leg.

She stepped away from the porch, put her hands on her knees, and took a few deep breaths.

A moment later, chaos erupted as people who'd heard the gunshot rushed toward her.

Kaylee realized she was on the ground, cold damp seeping through her clothes. Jessica bent over her, gripping her hand and calling her name.

"Wake up, Kaylee. Everything's okay now."

Kaylee opened her eyes. "Chad?"

"He can't hurt you."

Kaylee followed Jessica's gaze to the porch steps. Chad moaned as Sylvia Rosenthal tied her scarf around his leg. Her sister held the revolver on him.

"Do you think Penelope knows how to use that thing?" Kaylee whispered.

"I wouldn't try to take it away from her," Jessica said, with a concerned smile. "What happened, Kaylee?"

"Chad killed Jake. He said Jake killed Derek Glasser."

Kaylee tried to sit up, but Jessica pushed her back down. "Hear that? The ambulance is almost here. You're staying right where you are until you get checked out."

Sure enough, the sound of sirens grew as the vehicle neared. And not just the ambulance. The sirens from several sheriff's department vehicles also broke the peaceful quiet of the street.

"I'm fine, Jess."

"Not until the EMTs say you are."

Kaylee gave up. Besides, even with the cold and damp, there was something comforting about lying on the ground with her best friend instead of being in her SUV with a gun-toting killer. She gave a grateful sigh, then closed her eyes.

An image of Gina grieving at Jake's funeral slipped into her mind and chased away Kaylee's momentary contentment.

The only man Gina could ever count on, her brother, had murdered her husband. How would Kaylee help Gina survive this latest tragedy?

22

Kaylee sat in her favorite chair near the fire, wrapped in an afghan and sipping a cup of tea. Bear snuggled beneath the cover, pressing his warm body against her leg. It didn't seem right being home instead of at The Flower Patch, but despite her insistence that she was fine and had a lot of work to do, the Petal Pushers had ordered her to go home. Kaylee hadn't been able to resist their united front, especially after Sheriff Maddox added his unasked-for agreement.

After Kaylee told the sheriff about Chad's confession and his crazy plan, Robyn had driven her home. Whitney was still there, but Robyn insisted Kaylee rest while she filled Whitney in on what had happened. But after Whitney went into hysterics, Kaylee decided they all needed a cup of tea, so she made some.

That had been a couple of hours ago. After pulling herself together, Whitney joined Kaylee in front of the fire. Robyn worked on her laptop in the dining room while they waited for the sheriff to arrive. Kaylee hadn't thought Robyn needed to stay, but as she stared into the fireplace, she was glad the deputy was nearby. For one thing, Robyn had dealt with Whitney when Kaylee didn't have the emotional energy to do so. She'd thank her for that favor later. Perhaps with a bouquet of pink-and-white *Amaryllis belladonna*.

Jessica arrived first, driving Kaylee's SUV, which she'd filled with a cooler of sandwiches and snacks. Sheriff Maddox was right behind her. Whitney and Robyn joined Jessica in the kitchen so Sheriff Maddox could talk to Kaylee in private.

"How's Chad?" she asked as the sheriff lowered himself

into a chair.

"From the way he's carrying on, you'd think he was at death's door. But the bullet barely grazed his shin. It could have been worse."

"I'm glad he's not seriously hurt."

"He's claiming you shot him."

"All I did was knock him out."

"Good thing you did." He grinned fondly. "I'm not ready to lose my favorite forensic botanist."

Kaylee returned his smile, then took another sip of her tea as she stared at the dancing flames. He let her think for a few moments. Finally, she asked, "What will happen to him?"

"He'll be going away for a long time. You won't have to worry about him anymore."

"I still don't understand why he told me all that stuff about Jake. He didn't have to."

"Murder is an interesting thing," the sheriff said. "Not too many people have it in them to kill someone and keep it to themselves. Some just need to brag about it. Others feel a strong urge to confess. He thought he could unburden himself because he planned to kill you too."

"I wish he'd chosen someone else to bare his soul to. But that would have meant that he planned to kill that person instead, and they might not have been as lucky as I was." She glanced toward the sound of the women's voices in the kitchen. "As lucky as I am," she corrected herself.

They shared another short silence before Kaylee asked, "Do you think he's right? Did Jake kill Derek?"

"He did. Whitney saw the whole thing and finally told me about it last night. It terrified her. That's why she convinced her parents to skip town right after. When I talked to Gina this afternoon, she said Jake had convinced her that she was a suspect in Derek's death and offered to be her alibi. Poor girl didn't realize until we were talking that by letting Jake be her false alibi, she was also his."

"How is she?"

"Better than I would have expected. Everything about her life has been turned upside down, but she's not falling apart."

"But she will." Whitney leaned against the doorframe. "And when she does, I'll be there for her."

She entered the room and took a seat on the hearth, wrapping her arms around her legs. "I didn't mean to interrupt. Just wanted you to know that the food's ready whenever you are."

"You'll help Gina?" Kaylee asked, surprised.

"I owe her that. If I had told the truth back then, maybe Jake wouldn't have managed to charm her into marrying him. I'm not sure whether he did it as a strange way to get back at me for leaving or to solidify Gina into acting as his alibi."

"What happened that night?" Kaylee couldn't help asking.

Whitney took a deep breath. "Jake and I met on the pier for one of our secret dates. He handed me a few jasmine flowers and said he had something to show me at the marina. We were about to head that way when Derek rowed up in his skiff and saw us. He started yelling about how he thought I was his girl, and Jake told him to get lost because he had Gina. Derek grabbed my arms and shook me, which ruined the flowers, and Jake pushed between us and shoved Derek backward off the pier." Whitney paused and swallowed hard.

How awful.

"Derek hit his head really hard on his boat and went completely still. Jake grabbed my hand and pulled me away, telling me he was sure Derek was just unconscious and would come to in a few minutes. I asked if we should tell the sheriff or Derek's parents or something, so someone knew where he was, but Jake told me we couldn't tell *anyone*. He swore me to secrecy. And that's when I started to wonder if it had really been an accident. When they found Derek dead, I didn't care whether it was an accident or not. I couldn't stay in this town another minute."

"I don't blame you," Kaylee said. "Did you ever find out what he wanted to show you at the marina?"

"I checked into the circumstances of his buying Abner Murphy's boating business," Sheriff Maddox cut in. "It was a few days before Derek's death. My guess is that he wanted to show off his new business. I imagine he'd put the flower trail in place as a proposal and meant to go along with you as you followed the clues, Whitney. And he probably left it hidden in his desk because he didn't have the heart to get rid of it yet, though I'm sure he never meant Gina to find it. After all, it's not like he could have predicted his own murder. I'm sure he thought he'd get around to it someday."

Whitney nodded. "That sounds like him." She gazed at Kaylee with large, tear-filled eyes. "I'm so sorry I've been rotten to you since I got to town. It's just been so hard to be here."

Kaylee touched Whitney's arm. "I wasn't much better, and I'm sorry too. Friends?"

Whitney smiled. "Friends."

The Tuesday before Christmas, the Petal Pushers, their families, Reese, and the other residents of Turtle Cove gathered at the Old Cape Lighthouse beside an enormous Douglas fir that was decorated with gold and silver ornaments.

Sylvia and Penelope stood farther back, lips pursed and arms